TAROT FANTASIES PRIDE COLLECTION

5 LGBTQ+ BOOKS

JAX WILDER

TAROT FANTASIES PRIDE COLLECTION
COLLECTION

5 LGBTQ+ BOOKS

JAX WILDER

RAINBOW QUARTZ PUBLISHING

Published by Rainbow Quartz Publishing, Edmonds WA, 98026

First Edition: 2024 ISBN: 978-1-961714-70-0

Cover design by Miranda Townsend

Interior design by Miranda Townsend

Tarot Card description by Lorelai Hamilton from the book Teenage Tarot – used with permission.

For permissions or inquiries, please contact: Rainbow Quartz Publishing at rainbowquartzpublishing@gmail.com
RQPublishing.com

Jax Wilder

XII.

the Hanged Man

When Desire
Knows No
Bounds

Hanged
Passions

TAROT·FANTASIES
SERIES

HANGED PASSIONS

Tarot Fantasies Series
Jax Wilder

For every person who ever felt less than.
I see you, you sexy thing.
You are worthy of love.

Jax Wilder

12. THE HANGED MAN

"Shift your mindset and view the situation from a new angle," The Hanged Man.

Key Words and Phrases
Suspension and surrender
Seeing things from a new perspective
Letting go of control
Pause for reflection and introspection
Acceptance of delays or setbacks
Spiritual enlightenment and awakening
Release of old patterns or beliefs
Embracing the present moment

The Hanged Man is not struggling upside down. He's not freaking out. Considering everything, he seems pretty calm. He's completely at peace with his situation.

The Hanged Man is about gaining a new perspective. Sometimes you have to look at things from a different angle to really understand them. It's about shifting your mindset and seeing things in a whole new light.

It's not as easy as flipping yourself upside down and calling it a day. It's about surrendering to the moment, letting go of control, and trusting that everything will work out in the end.

The Hanged Man is also about sacrifice. Sometimes you have to give up something you want right now, for something even better in the future. It's all about patience and letting things unfold naturally.

Seeing this card in a reading is a reminder to take a step back, gain new perspective, and trust in the process. Sometimes the best thing you can do is hang tight.

—Lorelai Hamilton, author of *Teenage Tarot* and *Tarot Tales & Magic Spells*

THE HANGED MAN.

1

"Do you want to get out of here?" a husky voice with a cheeky smile asked.

I firmly grasped his muscular and well-defined arm, feeling the strength and power within it. "Yes," I said without thinking.

I had only been in this bar for about forty-five minutes, and I was already agreeing to go home with a guy? Not just any guy. This man was an absolute Adonis. Blond curly hair that was neat and trimmed above his beautiful deep blue eyes. Short, perfect button nose I wanted to bite.

"Do you want me to get us an Uber?" I asked as we walked onto the dirty street. The sound of car horns and the smell of exhaust wafted in the air.

"No need," Adonis said, grabbing my hand and leading me around the corner of the building. His hand was soft in mine. My cock swelled at his touch.

My gaze traveled up his arm, past his shoulders, and finally settled on his exposed, possibly shaved chest. If only my chest was as smooth as a polished stone. His nipples were perky and erect upon his bulky chest. I traced the curve of the valley between his well-defined pecs, my fingertips grazing his warm skin, until my hand reached the chiseled contours of his stomach. From there, my gaze followed the tantalizing "v" shape that swayed with his every step.

We turned down a dark alley. "Where are we heading?" I asked, meeting his eyes.

With a smile that revealed his pearly white teeth and luscious lips, Adonis motioned for me to follow him. "Just over here, handsome."

My mind drifted back to senior prom. I could still see the crowded hallways as couples filtered in. My heart pounded in my chest. The cutest guy in school wanted to be my date. I'd said yes, and when I arrived at prom, his sharp and cruel laugh still echoed in my ears. "You and me? You thought I was serious?" he sneered, eyes glancing around to make sure others were watching. "Not in a million years, Andrew." The humiliation burned just as fresh now as it did then, a constant reminder that people couldn't be trusted.

I willed the excitement coursing through me to stay the course and pushed thoughts of bullies aside. They had no control over me.

We tucked ourselves behind a large, green dumpster. With a sudden, swift motion, Adonis yanked me towards him, pinning me against the wall. His tongue entered my mouth, and I felt myself being pulled under, deeper and deeper. I kissed him back, running my hands up and down his perfectly sculpted chest. His hands traced the outside of my jeans, and his moans grew louder as he caressed my throbbing arousal.

I pulled back a little. "Where are we going to go?"

Adonis flashed another sly smile. "We're already here."

My gaze drifted down as he unbuttoned his white pants. He paused, surveying the alleyway from left to right. Our eyes locked, and in a bold move, Adonis firmly grasped my hand, leading it towards his cock.

The sensation of his throbbing erection

pressed against the fabric of his silky boxers was palpable. The tips of my fingers followed the outline of his shaft down towards his balls and massaged them gently. With an arched back, he leaned against the brick wall and rested his shoulder blades on it. I followed the outline of his cock back up towards the tip. Adonis closed his eyes, bit his bottom lip, and emitted a soft moan of pleasure.

"Oh yeah," his voice took on a deep, raspy quality.

My eyes traveled downward to his midsection, and he wasted no time in removing his blue, silky boxers, revealing his erect rod. He reached out and clasped his girth with his right hand, giving it a vigorous up and down.

I paused.

"Come on, you know you want it," he said as he arched back further. He shook his dick at me again.

Nervously, I glanced down the dimly lit alley, my eyes searching for any signs of movement on the street. Was this some kind of fucked-up joke? Anxiety gnawed at me relentlessly, pulling me from the inside. I looked down the opposite alley and saw a few people in the distance, obviously walking by, completely unaware of my existence. I couldn't shake the feeling that I was being punked. What did Adonis see in me?

I lowered myself to the ground, meeting his cock at eye level. He was still firmly clutched onto himself, waving his cock at my face.

"You want to suck that dick?" he asked as he bit his lip again.

I took his cock in my hands, feeling his smooth shaft. My hand replaced his. I glided my hand up and down. I glanced again down the alley, fear burning inside of me.

I brought my attention back to his perfectly chiseled body, my hand still gripping him. I leaned in and opened my mouth.

Licked my lips.

But then I let go and stood up. "I'm sorry. I can't do this. Not here," I said, walking away in the direction we came from. Although I could distinctly hear a sigh of frustration, there was no sound of him trailing behind me.

"The alleyway Adonis was two years ago?" Larissa blurted out in the middle of The Arcane Room.

"Shhhhh, Jesus Larissa, can you be any louder?"

I have been friends with Larissa since my freshman year of college. She was the first person I came out to, and she still embarrassed me on a near-daily basis.

"This is why we're here," Larissa blurts out, not even a decibel softer.

"To embarrass me?" I asked and felt my cheeks get hot.

"No, to release your inhibitions and free yourself!" Larissa spread her arms wide, nearly knocking over a bottle of green liquid off the shelf. "It's time to move on from the Seans and Adonises of the world."

Leave it to Larissa to bring up the most embarrassing moments of my life. Sean was my boyfriend in college. He wasn't out to his friends or family yet. I was standing in the middle of the room, a red solo cup in hand, when Sean approached me. We weren't public. He wouldn't hardly look at me when attending the same party. But that night had been different.

Sean was charming, flirty, and I was naive enough to believe his words. "I want you. I don't want to hide who I am anymore," he had said. My heart soared, but as soon as we stepped outside, his friends burst out laughing from behind the bushes.

"Did you really think he was into you?" they jeered. The shame of that moment still lingered, feeding my mistrust.

I centered myself and pushed the thoughts away. "I deserve better than assholes. I'm going to free my inhibitions or something." I forced a laugh.

"Damn right you are!" cheered Larissa.

Out of thin air, a mysterious woman suddenly emerged and swiftly snatched the jar out of thin air, preventing it from shattering.

"Freeing inhibitions? Sounds like you found the right place," the woman said with a warm smile.

I shot Larissa a look, my face flushed with embarrassment. "Sorry about that," I mumbled, trying to compose myself. "She can be a bit... enthusiastic."

The shop owner chuckled. Her eyes sparkled with amusement. "No need to apologize. Enthusiasm is welcome here."

Larissa grinned, clearly unfazed by my embarrassment. "See? I told you this place would be perfect for you."

The woman's gaze turned more curious. "So, what brings you to The Arcane Room today?"

I hesitated, glancing at Larissa for support. She nudged me forward, her eyes urging me to speak.

"I… I'm looking for guidance," I finally said, my voice barely above a whisper. "I've been feeling a little lost and stuck in my ways. Something has to change."

The woman nodded understandingly. She had long black hair and wore a flowing dress that accentuated her tattoos. "Follow me, dear." She led us to a counter near the back of the room. "Do you know much about tarot?"

"No," I admitted.

"Here at The Arcane Room, we offer a special…" she paused and met my eyes before continuing, "individualized experience."

She pulled out a deck of cards, much larger than a typical playing deck. She shuffled and laid them out on the table in front of me, backside up. "Choose only one," she said and waved her hand over the deck.

I glanced at Larissa, who nodded encouragingly. My hands trembled as I reached for a card, my mind racing with doubts. What if this was a mistake? What if I made a fool of myself again?

"The Hanged Man," Ms. Vesper breathed. "It represents suspension, letting go, and seeing things from a new perspective."

Her words struck a chord, but fear washed over

me. Letting go? I had spent my life trying to control how others saw me, building walls to protect myself. Could I really trust this process? My mind flashed back to the party in college, the punishing laughter of my ex's friends. I couldn't bear to be humiliated again.

It's also probably why I'm still single.

"The Hanged Man," she breathed. "It represents suspension, letting go, and seeing things from a new perspective. Sometimes, the only way to move forward is to stop struggling and simply surrender."

Her words resonated within me. A flicker of hope. "How do I do that?"

The woman stepped closer, her presence electrifying. "I can show you."

"Okay."

Before leading me into a small white room void of decor, she turned to Larissa. "I'll be right back out in a moment. Have a look around the store and I can answer any questions when I return."

Larissa spun on her heels and waved a hand in the air. "I'll just be out here, hitting on the next somethin'-somethin' that walks in."

She motioned for me to have a seat on the black leather chaise lounge in the center of the room.

From nowhere, she handed me a clipboard. "I just need you to sign this waiver and then we can begin."

I glanced at the waiver.

By participating, you accept that this simulation may involve physical and emotional sensations… I cocked my head but kept reading. *The experience includes drinking a special tea and a ritual spell casting by Ms. Vesper…* I looked up and she smiled back serenely. *Time within the simulation may feel longer than in reality, though the experience will only last twenty minutes in real-time. By participating, you release The Arcane Room and its staff from any liability for loss, damage, or injury that may occur.*

I gulped, wanting instinctually to leave out of fear. But Larissa trusted this woman. And I came looking to shake things up. So, I signed the waiver.

"I'm Andrew," I said, trying to steady my breathing and the pounding heart in my chest.

"Nice to meet you, Andrew," she took the form from me and passed me a cup of tea. Ms. Vesper smiled, her gaze intense and knowing. "You selected The Hanged Man. That tells me you're feeling trapped, unable to move forward. But it's more than that. You're inhibited by your fears and insecurities."

I nodded. "Something like that."

"This experience will help you release all of that anxiety you're carrying around so you can get to a place of," she sucked in a breath, "release."

"What exactly is going to happen?" I asked, trepidation evident in my voice.

"You'll drink that tea and then sit back and relax. Everything that happens beyond the tea is up to you. Remember, it's your fantasy, and you are the driver. The magic in this space will take you to a safe and wonderful place where you can live out your deepest and darkest inner desires."

"How much does all this cost?" I asked.

"It's not money that troubles me, but rather the negative energy swirling all around you. If you feel like your experience added something positive to your life, you are welcome to leave gratuity before you leave. Now drink up."

I looked down at the cup of tea in my hands, apprehension bubbling up in every inch of me. Ms. Vesper reached out and covered my hands, her touch sending a welcome shiver down my spine. "There is a path for you, and you will find it."

Her words filled me with hope. I can do this. I can let go. In several rapid gulps, I downed the tea.

"In the stillness of the night, The Hanged Man's strength, make clear his sight. Suspend fears, let wisdom flow. Through surrender, courage grows. Release doubts, let truth be known. Guide the path where light has shown." Ms. Vesper's voice was raw and laced with magic.

I slumped back into the chaise lounge as the room slipped away.

2

Squeezing my eyes shut, I waited for Ms. Vesper to provide me with instructions on what to do next. After some time passed, I peered through slits, before opening my eyes and looking around. Nothing. I was standing in the same white room.

No. Upon closer inspection, I noticed that this white room was significantly bigger than the one I initially entered. When I turned around to face the center, the black chaise had disappeared. I twirled around for a second time, expecting to see Ms. Vesper. She was not there.

"Hello?" I called out.

Where was the entrance? All four walls were identical. I looked up to realize that I was inside a pure white cage, the smooth white walls indistin-guishable from the floor and ceiling. It was disorienting.

"Hello?"

Without warning, something plummeted from above and crashed onto the floor. It was a man, a gorgeous man.

Suspended upside down, he dangled from the ceiling, the intricate knots of the ropes carefully wrapped around his body like a work of art. His skin was a smooth, sun-kissed bronze, muscles sculpted as if chiseled by a master artist. Every line, every curve of his body exuded strength and grace. With a broad chest that tapered down, his abs were like a symphony of ripples, moving with every breath he took.

I couldn't help but let my eyes trace the patterns of the ropes, each knot and twist accentuating his physique rather than hiding it. The ropes criss-crossed over his chest, snaked around his arms, and wound down his legs, creating a mesmerizing lattice that both restrained and highlighted his form. Despite the unconventional position, his legs remained strong and defined, and his feet seemed completely at ease.

Even inverted, his features were striking. High

cheekbones, a strong jawline, and full lips that seemed to invite attention. His eyes were closed, long dark lashes resting gently against his cheeks. His hair, a tousled dark mane, hung down towards the floor, adding to the surreal and hypnotic image before me.

My breath caught in my chest. I took him in inch by beautiful inch. With an air of tranquility, the man appeared to be completely at ease. It was second nature to him. The way he hung there, serene and composed, made it seem like he was an ethereal being, dropped into this realm from another.

My gaze traveled back up his body, lingering on the taut muscles of his arms and shoulders, the subtle flexing of his biceps as he maintained his balance. It was impossible to look away, every detail demanding attention, every inch of his skin drawing me in further.

Wandering up his body, I locked eyes on his exposed cock. Even in this upside-down state, it was impressive, his length hanging heavily, framed by the lines of the ropes. It was raw masculinity and vulnerable beauty. His cock was smooth and inviting.

The sheer audacity of his nakedness, coupled

with his serene confidence, made my pulse quicken. It was an intimate and erotic vision stirring a deep, primal response within me. I couldn't peel my eyes away.

"Hello, Andrew," the man said. The sudden break in silence startled me, and I stumbled backward, falling to a seated position on the floor.

"Uhh…," I stammered. "Hello. Sorry. Hello. I, uh…"

The naked man smiled. "You have no need for embarrassment here." His smile, albeit upside down, was assuring and warm.

"This is your fantasy, Andrew. You are always in control of what does or doesn't happen here. Nevertheless, it is important to acknowledge that your presence here signifies a willingness to surrender control. I will be your guide through all of this. You are safe. My name is Julian, and I am here for you," he said, his gaze never leaving mine.

"Nice to meet you," I said, looking around.

"It's just you and me here," Julian said, soothing my unease. "You are safe with me. Okay?"

I nodded.

"You are in control," Julian repeated. "For now. We'll take some of that control away after you and I are completely comfortable, but only when you ask me to, okay?"

I nodded again. "What do I do?"

"What do you want to do?" he asked.

I glanced over my shoulder, then back at Julian, still hanging from the ceiling. I noted his suspension point disappeared into the ceiling with no knots.

I shrugged.

"Why don't we start," he suggested with a mischievous grin, "by shedding those garments? How does that make you feel?" Julian asked.

Fidgeting with my T-shirt collar, I cast another quick glance around me.

"It's just you and I, Andrew," Julian assured me again.

I tugged at my shirt and pulled it off over my head. My body was a stark comparison to Julian's. His physique was a masterpiece, every muscle defined, his skin smooth and unmarred. Although my own chest felt inadequate, there was a certain sense of freedom in exposing myself to him.

I could see a faint outline of my ribs beneath my skin, a reminder of my lean frame. A rush of vulnerability and excitement, my heart pounding in my chest.

With a sigh of relief, I released the breath I had

been holding and gingerly reached for the waist-band of my jeans. Despite my fumbling fingers, I was able to successfully undo the button. With a deliberate motion, I eased my jeans down, relishing the sensation of the cool air caressing my skin. I stepped out of them, standing there in just my underwear, feeling exposed but strangely empowered.

Julian's intense gaze remained fixed on me, his eyes like magnets drawing me closer, captivated by his unwavering attention. His presence was magnetic, and I wanted to please him, to show him everything. With a final, deep breath, I hooked my thumbs into the waistband of my underwear and slid them down, stepping out of them. I stood completely nude.

I stirred under his gaze and imagined my body through Julian's eyes. The feeling was thrilling and intimidating, a mix of excitement and appre-hension.

There I stood, bare before him, my skin tingling with the coolness of the room and the heat of his eyes. Every inch of me on display, and for the first time, I felt a strange sense of liberation in my nudity.

"Why don't you step back over here, beautiful," Julian said.

A primal, animalistic lust shot through my veins. I moved forward.

"Closer."

Another step, and my face met his groin.

"Do you see how hard you make me?" he asked.

"Yes," I said, my mouth watering for his bulge.

"Do you want to put that in your mouth?" Julian asked, clearly knowing the answer already. "Be a good boy and take me whole."

I leaned forward, mouth opened and ready, and used my tongue to guide him inside of me without the use of my hands.

3

Julian was a burst of sweet and salty. I eagerly tasted every inch of his girth, relishing the sensation of every ridge and vein under my tongue. The sound of Julian's pleasure-filled moan fueled the fire of passion, pushing me deeper. Another thrust of my mouth before releasing his member. I spit on my hand, grabbed his cock, and stroked it slowly until it slipped easily between my fingers.

I eagerly took him back into my mouth, using the motion of my hand to heighten his pleasure. He let out a feral growl, which made me stroke him faster and harder. I squeezed harder to increase the pressure and felt him swell even more.

"Slow down, baby. We've got all the time in the

world," Julian whispered. I couldn't help it. I wanted to taste him completely. My mouth worked eagerly, savoring every moment. Julian's hand, now free, tangled in my hair, guiding me gently.

I pulled back slightly. In that fleeting moment, our eyes met, and it felt like time stood still. Julian's expression softened, his gaze full of warmth and desire. He cupped my face, his thumb tracing my lips.

"Let's take this slow," he murmured, his voice tender and sweet. He pulled his swinging body close to mine, the heat between us palpable. I met his lips and tasted the lingering sweetness of our kiss, savoring every second.

The awkwardness of him being upside down was growing apparent. "I think we're ready for the next level of intimacy. Give me a moment to get out of these ropes."

I took a step back, my eyes scanning the ceiling for any possible means to help him escape from his binds. There was no visible way to lower him to the ground and attempt to untangle the web that bound him. To my astonishment, I discovered him standing upright and unbound, with the ropes dangling loosely behind him as if they were mere afterthoughts.

"How did you…" I trailed off.

"Magic," he smiled coyly.

Julian reached for a hug. Closing the distance between us, he held me tightly in his arms. I melted between his powerful arms, feeling safe and desired. Something I'd never felt so wholly before. Julian's touch was gentle as he guided me. But my mind was a whirlwind of insecurity. What did Julian see in me? Did he notice the scars, the imperfections, the stretchmarks, and love handles?

"You're safe with me," Julian whispered, sensing my hesitation. "There's nothing here but acceptance."

I took a deep breath, feeling a flicker of hope. Julian's words soothed my fears. For the first time, I felt a glimmer of trust, a tentative step towards opening up. His eyes held a warmth that melted away the cold grip of my past. Maybe, just maybe, I could let someone in.

While we embraced each other, the walls of the room seemed to shimmer and shift. Out of nowhere, a door appeared, a seamless part of the white expanse just moments before. Julian gently released me, took my hand, and led me toward the door.

We stepped through the door. The next room

was a dark, rich red and black aesthetic. Luxurious fabrics draped the walls, absorbing the light and creating an intimate, almost mystical ambiance. In the center of the room was a large, comfortable-looking bed, its dark sheets and plush pillows inviting.

Julian's presence beside me was reassuring as I took in the new surroundings. The contrast between the stark white room and this dark, sensuous space was disorienting yet exhilarating.

"This is more like it," Julian said, his voice a low, seductive rumble. With a confident and fluid motion, he released his grip on my hand and gracefully made his way towards the bed. I followed, nervous anticipation bubbling inside me.

Julian turned to face me, his eyes gleaming with mischief. "Are you ready to continue our adventure?" he asked, voice charged with promise.

I nodded. The intimacy of the moment, the closeness we shared, and the thrill of the unknown all combined to create a heady mix of emotions.

Julian took my hand again, pulling me close. His lips, warm and insistent, locked with mine in a deep and passionate kiss. As our bodies pressed together, I could feel the tension and desire building between us. The world outside this dark, alluring room ceased to exist. There was only Julian and the promise of what lay ahead.

We moved towards the bed together, the soft fabric of the sheets brushing against my skin as we climbed into it. Julian's hands roamed over my body, his touch electrifying.

He paused, his eyes locking onto mine. "Let's take our time," he whispered, his breath hot against my ear. "We have all the time we want."

The promise in his words thrilled me. We lay there, wrapped in each other's arms. Anticipation was almost overwhelming. This was more than just physical. We connected. Deep and undeniable, forged in magic.

With my finger, I traced the outline of his face, gently tickling with every stroke. I ran my finger around his perfect lips until desire was exploding inside of me, demanding more. I grabbed a fistful of hair and pulled him into me. We kissed, our tongues battling each other for space. The intensity of his desire was evident by his swollen member, stabbing me in the stomach.

He pulled me closer, our lips pressed together. He pushed me flat on my back and climbed on top of me. I couldn't help but revel in the feeling of his weight pressing into me.

"Are you ready for the next exercise?" Julian asked, still on top of me.

His face radiated beauty, and I couldn't resist the urge to run my fingers through his hair, savoring the softness as I lovingly stroked his ear. I couldn't imagine how this could get any better, but I nodded, ready for whatever was next.

"No more kissing," he said and smirked.

Despite the sinking feeling in my stomach, I chose to trust him. "Okay?"

"We're going to take turns exploring each other's bodies with our hands. No kissing. No sucking. No penetration," Julian explained.

I grinned. "Who's first?"

4

Julian laid down on his stomach next to me. I turned onto my side, giving my right hand better access to his body. Anticipation coursed through my trembling fingers as they ventured across his broad back, tracing the contours of the firm muscle beneath his velvety skin.

Julian's skin radiated warmth under my touch. Using my fingertips, I delicately drew loops on his shoulders and followed the curves of his spine, paying attention to every rise and fall. His muscles relaxed beneath me, and I moved lower, letting my hand glide over his firm buttocks. I squeezed gently, marveling at the perfect firmness.

Continuing my exploration, I felt the strength of his powerful thighs beneath my hand. His legs exuded tension and power, the muscles rippling from his calves down to his feet. My fingers gently kneaded into the arch and toes of each foot, and Julian responded with soft, contented murmurs.

As I moved back up his legs, I couldn't help but be drawn to the curves of his ass again. Leaning in, I placed a soft kiss on the peak of his right cheek, tasting the salt of his skin. Suddenly, Julian tensed and turned his head slightly.

"Hands only, Andrew," he said firmly.

A wave of embarrassment washed over me, causing me to instinctively pull back. I'd broken the rules, so it was understandable. With a sigh, I released my breath and explored further, relying solely on the sensation of touch from my fingers. Taking in every inch of his body, memorizing the feel of his skin and the strength beneath it. The intimacy of the moment grew.

With each stroke, I could sense the steady ebb and flow of Julian's breath, syncing with my own. His contented sigh filled the room, as his body melted into an even deeper state of relaxation. I marveled at him, feeling a mixture of desire and admiration.

My hands moved back to the mounds of his ass, spreading his cheeks apart while I stuck my finger down his hairless crack. When I reached his hole, I gently massaged the outside with the tip of my middle finger. Julian flinched and his cheeks clamped down around my finger.

"Hey. I thought I was allowed as long as it was my hands," I said, my voice filled with the disappointment of a child who was just denied their favorite toy.

"Oh, it's allowed," Julian laughed, "but I'm also very sensitive, and that was a completely involuntary clench."

"I see," I smirked and spread his ass even more open, exposing his hole to me. His anus, tight and inviting, drew me in. It was a point of both vulnerability and desire, a hidden pleasure waiting to be discovered. My finger hovered just above, feeling the heat emanating from him and the anticipation between us.

The tip of my finger outlined his hole once more, and he squirmed and moaned beneath my touch. This made me swell.

I wanted more.

With his cheeks spread open, I leaned in and spit just above his rosebud. The bead slipped down into his hole. I inserted the tip of my finger slowly, pulling out to allow more moisture inside. With a gentle touch, I slid my finger inside him, stopping when I made it to the first knuckle. He was warm and smooth, like a silk pillow. He let out a deep moan that verged on a growl. I continued further to the next knuckle. His hole tightened around my finger.

The more I pressed, the more I could sense the intense heat and tautness of his body completely enveloping my finger. Julian's moans grew louder, more desperate, as I explored him with a slow, deliberate rhythm. His reactions fueled my desire, and I found myself lost in the moment, captivated by the intimacy of this connection.

Julian's back arched slightly, his muscles tensing and relaxing in response to my touch. I could feel the raw need radiating from him, and it spurred me on, making me want to pleasure him. In every movement, I listened to his body to understand what he needed.

I added another finger, slowly stretching him, preparing him. In that moment, Julian's breath hitched, and a deep, resonant moan escaped him, electrifying the air between us. I leaned in, my lips brushing against the small of his back, and felt him shiver beneath me.

"Watch those lips, Andrew," he murmured, and

I backed off. He arched his back, allowing my fingers deeper inside of him. "More, please."

I obliged, working my fingers deeper, feeling his body's response to my touch. The restrictions placed upon me were driving me insane. Desire surged through me, intensifying with every passing second.

Julian's hips moved in time with my fingers, his body seeking more pleasure. I could tell he was close, the tension in his muscles reaching a peak. I wanted to bring him to the edge, to watch him experience the cliffs of pleasure.

Just as I was about to send him over the edge, Julian's eyes locked onto mine, filled with a raw, primal hunger. "Stop." His voice was firm but gentle. "Not yet."

I withdrew my fingers slowly, feeling the loss of warmth around them. Julian rolled onto his back, panting. His chest heaved with deep breaths. He pulled me down beside him, wrapping me with his arms.

"That was amazing," he whispered, his lips brushing against my ear. "But there's so much more I want to do with you."

5

"It's your turn," Julian whispered, his lips barely grazing against my ear. With a gentle touch, he laid me down on my back and carefully positioned my arms above my head. "Get comfortable, but don't move."

I complied, feeling a surge of anticipation. I laid there, exposed and waiting for his touch. Julian's eyes devoured my body, a hungry glint in his gaze that sent a chill through my stomach. His hands were warm as they began their journey, starting at my neck.

He traced a line down my throat, his touch feather-light and teasing. My pulse quickened. His fingers moved lower, over my collarbones, and then spread out to my shoulders. His touch left me aching for more.

Julian's fingers danced over my chest, weaving through the hair that covered it. He played with my hair, tugging lightly, before moving on. His fingers grazed my nipples. I gasped as he pinched one, sending a jolt of pleasure straight to my groin.

Julian smirked, clearly enjoying the effect it had on me. "Stay still," he reminded me softly, his breath hot against my skin.

His hands trailed down, grazing my ribs before settling on my stomach. Julian took his time exploring the trail of hair that led from my navel south. He traced the line with his fingers, skirting around my cock, which strained with need.

My breath hitched as his hands traveled over my hips and down my thighs. He massaged the muscles there, his fingers digging in just enough for a groan to escape me. Julian's hands gently glided from my knees to my calves, their touch evoking a tender sensation that quickened my heartbeat.

Despite his demand to stay still, I found it increasingly challenging to resist the urge to move. His hands were everywhere, teasing and tantalizing, but never touching where I needed it most. My body was on fire, every nerve ending screaming for his touch.

Julian's hands moved to my feet, outlining every toe. He dragged his tip across my arches. I squealed and pulled back involuntarily at this. The sensation was maddening.

"Don't. Move," Julian playfully barked.

I released my knees and laid my legs back flat against the bed. Desire pooled in my stomach, a burning need that grew with each passing second. Julian worked his hands back up my legs and drew into my inner thigh. I wanted to squirm, but held strong—just as I was told.

"Julian," I whispered, my voice shaky. "Please…"

A wicked grin played at his lips. "Patience, Andrew," he tsked. "We're just getting started."

With deliberate slowness, he caressed my thighs, my calves, my ankles. Each touch sent sparks of pleasure through me. When he reached my hips, he traced around my cock, raking his fingers through my bush, gently scratching at the skin.

Finally, he brought his hands to my face, cradling it gently. He leaned down and held his lips above mine, his breath and the warmth of him hovering above me. I wanted to arch my neck off the pillow to meet his lips with mine, but somehow, I resisted the temptation. He outlined my lips with the tip of his finger, never pulling his face away from mine. Desire burned in his eyes, their depths filled with darkness and longing.

"I want you to remember every touch," he whispered. "Every moment."

I nodded, my heart pounding in my chest. Julian smiled and then began his teasing all over again, his hands exploring my body with a skill and tenderness that left me breathless.

"Flip over onto your stomach," Julian demanded.

I did as I was told. I adjusted my stiff cock to rest between my stomach and the warm mattress underneath.

Julian started at my shoulders, applying firm pressure to my muscles. His touch eased away any tension. He worked his way down my back, melting away any stress.

Julian's hands moved skillfully over my buttocks, applying a firm yet sensual pressure. His fingers kneaded the muscles, coaxing them to relax under his skilled touch. He placed soft kisses along the path.

"Hey, I thought it was hands only?" I pouted.

"Are you upset?" he teased.

"Absolutely not," I said, matching his energy.

"Good. Now be quiet and don't interrupt me, boy."

His forceful command did strange things to me. His words were uncomfortable, but somehow liberating. I can't describe why or what, but I knew one thing. I wanted more.

"Flip over," Julian commanded, and I complied, shifting on my back. He moved gracefully, his hands gliding over my body with a practiced ease.

He took my nipple in his mouth. My body quivered with delight as he gently sucked on my nipple, sending waves of pleasure pulsating through me. His teeth grazed my nipple with a gentle bite.

I let out an impulsive scream.

He stopped. "Are you okay?"

Gasping for air, I fought to find my voice and respond. I nodded. "Oh, yeah."

Julian smirked and moved to the other nipple. The sting of the bite sent a jolt of pain through my body, and I narrowly stifled another scream. I had never felt such a pleasurable pain.

As Julian completed the massage portion, he sat back on his knees, his gaze meeting mine with a soft, reassuring smile. His hands rested lightly on my skin, a silent gesture of comfort and care. "How are you feeling?" he asked gently, his voice warm with concern.

"Amazing," I said with a sigh.

"I think you're ready for the next step," Julian said.

"Absolutely," I exclaimed, having no idea what was in store, but with Julian, I didn't care.

Julian's eyes sparkled with mischief. "The next step," he murmured, "is trust. Complete trust."

I swallowed hard, nodding. "I trust you."

He smiled warmly. "Good. Then close your eyes and let go."

6

J ulian's command was clear and assertive, sending a thrill through me. "Spread your legs," he said.

I obeyed without hesitation, spreading my legs wider, offering myself completely to him.

"Good boy."

His words sent an explosion inside of my stomach, and I bit my lip to stifle a moan.

"You like that, don't you?" Julian asked, his voice soft yet commanding.

"Uh huh," I nodded, feeling a mixture of vulnerability and desire.

"When I call you a good boy?"

"Uh huh."

Julian wiggled his fingers as he moved slowly up my inner thighs, setting me ablaze. I moaned softly, the anticipation building with each touch. Julian paused and delicately tugged at my balls, sending pleasurable sensations radiating through my groin. He grabbed both with a single hand and stroked them in his palm, using his free fingers to tickle at the area just under my sack.

This made me squirm and open my legs wider to offer myself completely to him. He ran his hand back up my sack to the base of my shaft, tickling at the hair as he passed. He grabbed at my girth and slowly stroked, pulling my skin along.

I whimpered with pleasure, my hips pulsing in time with his strokes. Gently, with two fingers, he pulled my foreskin up over the tip and rolled it back down again. He repeated this action tirelessly, exerting a precise pressure that pushed me to the brink.

Before I could get there, he let go and my dick made a loud 'thwap' as it landed back on my stomach. Julian licked at my sack, sending tingles up my spine. He greedily sucked one inside his warm, wet mouth. He rolled it around, applying pressure between his tongue and the roof of his mouth.

Gently, he released it and did the same with my left nut. I squirmed on the inside, but was careful not to move away from him. I didn't want him to stop.

"That feels amazing," I assured him.

"You don't need to tell me. Your body is showing me," Julian explained. "Don't talk unless I tell you to."

I almost spoke to say, "Yes sir," but nodded instead.

"Good boy," he said and winked at me.

I threw my head back in pleasure at his words. He skillfully deepthroated my entire cock, leaving me gasping for breath. I nearly threw my back out, arching into him. As he took me all the way in, I could feel the tip brushing against the back of Julian's throat. His throat squeezed around me and I pulled out a little to provide him with relief.

To my surprise, he pulled me back in. The tightness pulsating on the edge of my cock was nearly too much. He backed out and then back in again, sending my middle into a frenzy.

A few more strokes and an explosion was forming deep within my sack. He slowly retreated, denying me the chance to find release.

I let out an exasperated sigh.

"It's not time yet, Andrew," Julian said. "We haven't begun the next level yet."

This surprised me. How much further could we go? I was about to give him my hot load directly into his throat.

"Sit up for me and lean back on the head of the bed," Julian commanded.

I did as I was told. Julian handed me a pillow to place in the small of my back. After I was comfortable, Julian spread my legs just wide enough so that he could sit in between them on his knees, his entire beautiful body exposed to me.

"I want you to take care of yourself," Julian said.

"How so?"

"I want to know what makes you tick," Julian explained. "We're going to be more verbal now. I'm going to tell you what I want you to do to yourself, and you're going to tell me what to do."

I smiled. "Okay. Grab your cock," I demanded.

"As you wish," Julian said. He grabbed his cock with his right hand. His girth filled his palm, and I raised my hand out to join him. He slapped it away.

"Nope, you want me to do something? You need to tell me, and I'll do it myself," Julian said.

"Okay, grab my hand and place it on your dick," I smiled with a cheeky grin.

"Haha, you're missing the point," Julian said.

"No, I'm not. I was trying to be funny," I smiled. "Stroke it for me."

Julian adhered to my command and started stroking himself. Long strokes that started at the base of his shaft and slowly moved out to the head, adding a little twist to the end, where the head meets the shaft. His twisted stroke left his cock, leaving his hand entirely. Julian used the head to break open the pressure that had formed by his closed fist. The stroke unfurled as it went slowly back down the shaft.

I licked my lips as I watched him. His eyes were locked onto me, stroking.

"Rub your other hand on your chest while you continue stroking," I ordered.

"Yes, Sir," Julian heeded. A hand met his navel and moved between his pecs. He gently caressed his right pec, his hand following the curves of his muscles around and around. His fingers gently brushed over his nipples in a circular motion.

His member stiffened with each stroke. His index finger and thumb worked gently at his left nipple, and he arched his back and sat up taller on his knees and locked eyes with me. He bit his lip, softly moistening his lips as he moaned.

"You like that?" he asked. The long strokes from his right hand continued.

"You are beautiful," I said, enjoying my show.

Julian smiled and then turned it on me. "Now, it's your turn. Show me how you like it."

I grabbed at myself and started stroking. To my delight, Julian never stopped stroking himself. I started stroking my tip almost exclusively, only every few strokes going the length of my shaft. Julian studied my cock and hand motions.

With my free hand, I began to tease and finger at my hole, intensifying the pleasure with each stroke. I adjusted my position so that my ass was more exposed for easier access. After moistening my fingers with spit, I carefully returned it to my hole. I ran my fingers along the circumference before sliding one inside. I remembered that this was the same finger that was inside of Julian, and it made me even more excited.

I moaned loudly.

"You like that, don't you?" Julian asked.

I nodded, barely able to speak with all of my senses alight.

"You're such a good boy, aren't you?" he asked.

"Oh fuck yes," I said, nodding slowly. This man learned all of my triggers just to exploit them.

"Are you ready for the next level, then?"

"Fuck yes," I begged.

7

Julian pulled out a large box from the bedside table. It matched the theme of the room, mostly black with red metallic accents. He lifted the lid carefully and asked, "Do you trust me?"

"I do," I replied.

Julian pulled out ropes and laid them in front of me. My heart raced with nerves. Julian must have sensed my distress because he stopped unpacking the ropes.

"We don't have to do anything you're not comfortable with," he reassured.

"I know. I want to," I said.

"I'm glad to hear it," he smiled, and I melted.

Any fear I had melted with it. Once again, my heart raced, but this time it was with excitement.

Julian took the first set of ropes and gently guided my arms above my head. He secured one wrist, his fingers working deftly as he tied the knots firmly. He moved to the other wrist, his touch careful and considerate.

"How does that feel?" he asked, his voice soothing.

"Good," I said, testing the bonds. They were secure but not painful, allowing a slight range of motion.

Julian moved to my feet, wrapping the ropes around each ankle and securing them to the corners of the bed. As he worked, he maintained eye contact, ensuring I was comfortable every step of the way.

"Remember, if at any point you want to stop, just say the word," he said.

"I will," I promised, appreciating the concern.

With my limbs bound, Julian leaned back, admiring his work. He then climbed onto the bed beside me, his hands gently tracing the ropes on my skin.

He worked his way down to my stomach, hands moving in slow, purposeful circles. I closed my eyes, losing myself to the sensation. He moved to my arms, massaging from my shoulders down to my wrists, carefully around the ropes. He took his time, ensuring every inch of my skin was attended to.

A surge of warmth and comfort moved through me, knowing I was in safe hands. Julian's presence was reassuring, his touch exhilarating. He leaned in closer, gently kissing my neck.

"You're doing great," he whispered. "Just relax and enjoy."

I let out a contented sigh, surrendering to the moment. The world outside ceased to exist, and all that mattered was Julian and his touch.

Julian continued to move his hands skillfully over my body, his touch tender and firm. He ran his fingers through my chest hair, tugging gently. He moved back up to my shoulders, working out my knots with practiced ease, sending waves of relaxation and desire through me.

His hands traveled down my sides, each touch barely a graze against the sensitive skin there. I squirmed. The sensation was extremely ticklish. I caught myself sucking in and holding my breath.

Julian's smooth voice calmed me. "Just breathe, Andrew," he whispered, lips close to my ear. "Let go."

I obeyed, focusing on my breath, letting the air in my chest melt away. Julian's hands moved lower, massaging my thighs with a firm but gentle grip. He worked each muscle with care, his touch knowing and skilled.

He let up the pressure and started tickling at my feet. Unable to recoil from his attacks, I arched my back as far as I could, laughing and squirming. Julian kept at it and smiled with delight.

Julian paused at my middle, leaning in to kiss the shaft of my cock, then moved down and kissed each of my balls. He then rubbed his five o'clock shadow against the sensitive skin of my hard-on. Each kiss and movement was soft, almost reverent. A pulsating rush of pleasure ran up and down my spine.

He opened his mouth, licked my tip, and took me all the way inside his mouth. He thrust gently and swiftly, focusing concertedly on the tip. I squirmed once again, which made him take me in deeper.

Julian gently let me go and ran his tongue down the length of my shaft to my sack. He ran his tongue back and forth between my two stones until they were wet with his moisture. Contained by the ropes, I arched my body, feeling the tension in every muscle.

His rough stubble grazed my skin, causing me to let out an unexpected squeal of delight.

"Mmmm, someone liked that, huh?" Julian asked.

"Yes, sir." I arched off the bed, exposing my ass to him.

Julian let out a menacing growl and sank his body lower onto the bed. He arched his body into an inner thigh stretch between my legs, his shoulders pinning my thighs as wide as they could go with my ankles restrained. He wrapped his arms underneath me so that my ass was lifted off the bed and completely exposed to him.

Julian's hands rested on the top of my legs. He tickled close to my sack with his tongue. I squirmed. There was no way for me to move, except for scooting my ass closer to his face. His lips gently brushed against the sensitive skin of my lower inner thigh.

"Eat that ass," I said.

"Beg me." Julian kissed at my inner thigh again, this time on my left side.

"Please."

"What?"

"Please sir, eat that ass," I begged.

"You want me to eat this ass?" He kissed my exposed hole.

"Oh fuck yes, please."

Julian moved in closely, positioning his face near my ass as his tongue expertly explored every inch, paying particular attention to my crack. I let out a loud moan and felt my dick swell. I could feel his tongue gently exploring my entrance. His stubble rubbing against my split. Determined, I attempted to lower myself even more onto his face, seeking a better position.

His tongue punched at my hole, and I relaxed to let it inside. He moved it rhythmically while inside of me, and a flash of ecstasy filled my center.

I screamed out. "I need you now. Please, take me!"

A mischievous grin stretched across Julian's face. "Now we're talking."

8

Julian sat up in the bed and adjusted himself to his knees. He grabbed at his engorged shaft and slapped it against mine.

"Is this what you want?" he teased.

"Yes, please," I cried.

"You want this inside of you?" he jiggled his thick, veiny rod up and down and slapped it against my thigh.

"Please, I need you. I can't take it anymore, please. Please, sir," I begged.

Leaning over me, his face loomed inches away from mine. "You're a good boy, and I love how good you beg for this cock," he said, and he kissed me. I took him in, feeling his body against mine.

"Fuck me, please," I truly begged this time. The suspense was too much to bear.

Julian let his heat-seeking missile find my hole. Then, gently, he forced his way inside. My head shot backward as the initial shock set in. He held position while my body adjusted to his bulging cock.

"You doing okay?" he asked, looking for reassurance.

"Fuck yes." I shifted to take him in deeper.

"You are quite the eager one, aren't you?" he smiled his saucy grin.

I nodded.

He slid in further.

I gasped as I took him all the way inside of me. Julian held once more. Once my stomach had relaxed again, he thrusted. With slow, deliberate movements, he moved inside me. In and out. My eyes rolled back into my head, overwhelmed by the intensity.

He thrusted inside of me, his sack clapping against me. I screamed out in pleasure as I took him in, repeatedly. I wished I could reach down and stroke my cock as he pumped deeper and deeper inside of me.

Then, as if he was reading my thoughts, he reached down and grabbed ahold of my girth, stroking me with careful consideration of the head. My breathing quickened. I felt an explosion building from inside of me. I held my breath. He thrust harder and stroked me faster.

He licked his other hand, spit filling his palm. Switching hands, he continued stroking me. Julian's breath became more labored, matching my own.

Faster.

And faster.

My breath was stolen from me. The explosion inside of me was too much to hold on to. I let out a primal howl as my release erupted, splattering across my chest and stomach. Julian continued stroking. My body convulsed uncontrollably. The cascading fluid dripped down his knuckles while he thrusted inside me.

Two more thrusts and his head flew back in exultation, his heat exploding inside of me. Julian's body quivered with excitement, and he let out a primal growl of pleasure. When he could breathe normally again, he looked down at his knuckles covered in my juices. He delicately licked his finger, removing every trace of my cum.

He pulled himself from me and collapsed on top of me. Our combined moisture flowed together in a cold soup between our hot skin. We both writhed and shook as the aftershocks of pleasure rocked through our bodies. He kissed me, and I tasted myself on his tongue, sweet and tangy.

Julian flopped down beside me, running his hands over my nipples and through my chest hair. His right leg draped over my body, wrapping me in an embrace.

"I'm so proud of you. You were amazing," he whispered in my ear.

I wanted to hold him, but my hands and feet were still bound. I was completely helpless and vulnerable to him.

Julian noticed my struggle and chuckled softly. "Let me take care of that," he said, reaching for the knots that held me captive. His fingers worked expertly, and soon the ropes fell away, freeing me from my restraints.

I flexed my wrists and ankles, feeling the circulation return. Julian's hands moved gently, massaging the areas where the ropes had been, soothing the slight soreness.

"Thank you," I purred, wrapping my arms around him now that I could. The sensation of his warm body against mine was comforting.

Intimate.

He kissed my forehead tenderly, his lips

lingering for a moment before he found my eyes. "You're welcome," he purred with a soft smile. "It was an incredible experience."

We lay there for a while, enjoying the closeness and the shared warmth. The night was quiet, the room dimly lit by the soft glow of the bedside lamp. Julian and I lay there, our bodies intertwined. The intensity of the evening had given way to a peaceful stillness, a perfect moment to reflect on everything that had happened.

"You know," Julian began, his voice gentle, "the voices from our past only have the power we give them."

I turned to face him, his words striking a chord deep within me. "What do you mean?"

Julian squeezed my hand, his eyes searching mine. "Those moments of hurt and rejection, they don't define you unless you let them. You've been carrying memories like weights, but you don't have to. You can choose to let them go."

I felt a lump form in my throat as his words sank in. "It's hard," I admitted. "Those voices, they've been with me for so long."

Julian nodded, understanding in his eyes. "I know it's not easy. But look at how far you've come. You've faced your fears, opened up, and let someone in. That's growth, Andrew. You're stronger than you think."

I thought back to all the moments of vulnerability, the times I wanted to run but stayed. The echoes of high school rejection, the humiliation from college, Adonis in the alleyway, they felt distant now, like shadows losing their grip.

"You're right," I said softly. "I've been letting those voices control me for too long."

Julian smiled, a warmth that reached his eyes. "You have the power to rewrite those narratives. To see yourself not through their eyes, but through your own. Through mine."

I took a deep breath, feeling a weight lift off my shoulders. "Thank you, Julian. For everything."

He leaned in, pressing a gentle kiss to my forehead. "You did this, Andrew. You found the strength within yourself. I'm just here to remind you of what you're capable of."

As we lay there, the past no longer felt like a chain holding me down. Instead, it was a part of my story, one that I could learn from and move beyond. I knew the journey wasn't over, but for the first time, I felt a sense of peace. A belief in my own strength and worth.

"I'm ready," I whispered, more to myself than to Julian. "I'm ready to let go."

Julian's smile widened, his eyes shining with pride. In that moment, I knew I was no longer defined by the voices of my past. I was defined by the choices I made, the love I embraced, and the strength I found within myself. And with Julian by my side, the future felt brighter than ever.

Eventually, Julian sighed and sat up. "I suppose it's time to say goodbye," he said, a hint of reluctance in his voice.

I nodded, feeling a pang of sadness but also a sense of fulfillment. "Until next time," I replied.

Julian leaned in for one last kiss, slow and lingering, savoring the moment. "Until next time," he echoed, his eyes filled with promise.

With a final smile, he stood up and started dressing. I followed suit, the weight of the experience sinking into my bones and etching itself into a treasured memory.

"Take care, Andrew," he breathed.

"You too, Julian." I walked out of the room feeling a mixture of exhilaration, contentment, and sorrow. Already looking forward to the next encounter, I wondered if I truly would ever see him again. The white room got brighter and brighter until the brightness blinded me completely.

9

I gently opened my eyes and found myself in the small white room, laying on the black chaise. My return to The Arcane Room was disorienting and peaceful all at the same time. A small rush of embarrassment flooded through me when I remembered I had Larissa to contend with in the next room. She would ask me every detail of my encounter.

The memory of Julian's words resurfaced, emphasizing the exclusivity of our experience—it was something shared only between us. I relaxed.

"So, how was it?" Ms. Vesper asked with a sly smile.

I hadn't realized she was there. "Incredible." I couldn't contain the ear-to-ear smile. As we exited the white room and walked back into the main part of the store, I saw Larissa.

Before she interjected, I asked, "How much do I owe you?"

Ms. Vesper chuckled, a mischievous glint in her eyes. "The first time is free, but gratuities are always welcome."

I nodded, feeling grateful. I reached into my wallet and handed her a generous tip. "Thank you, Ms. Vesper. It was truly an unforgettable experience."

Larissa was waiting for me, her eyes wide with curiosity. "Wow, you look… different," she remarked, tilting her head. "What happened in there?"

I gave her a knowing smile. "It's your turn to find out," I said, gesturing towards the table with the tarot deck.

Her eyes lit up with excitement and a bit of apprehension. "Really? You think I should?"

"Absolutely," I encouraged her. "It's an experience you don't want to miss."

Ms. Vesper stepped forward, placing a comforting hand on Larissa's shoulder. "Ready to explore, my dear?"

Larissa glanced at me one last time before nodding eagerly. "Okay, let's do this."

As Ms. Vesper guided Larissa toward the table, I watched them go, feeling a sense of satisfaction. The Arcane Room had already changed my life, and I knew it was about to do the same for Larissa.

Julian's words and the journey we'd shared had given me a fresh perspective. I knew that this was just the beginning of a new chapter in my life, one where I embraced my true self and let go of the past.

The Arcane Room had opened a door within me, and I was eager to walk through it, knowing that I was no longer bound by the shadows of my past.

Sign up for Jax Wilder's newsletter and receive a collection of unpublished Coral Cove short stories. Meet familiar characters and dive deeper into the love and romance that Coral Cove is known for. Don't miss out on this exclusive content!

Jax Wilder

You can also join Rainbow Quartz Publishing's Newsletter:

Rainbow Quartz Publishing

Jax Wilder

Three of Cups

Tarot Fantasies Series

THREE OF CUPS

Tarot Temptations Series

For Amanda

3 OF CUPS

"Let us raise our cups high in celebration, as we dance in harmony and embrace the beauty of togetherness," 3 of Cups.

KEY WORDS AND PHRASES:

Celebration and joyous gatherings
Friendship and camaraderie
Reunion with loved ones
Shared happiness and mutual support
Socializing and bonding with others
Emotional fulfillment and contentment
Expressing gratitude and appreciation
Festivities and good times
Community and belonging

Harmonious relationships and connections

The Three of Cups is a symbol of celebration—it's all about coming together with friends and having a good time.

Picture a moment of celebration, three cups raised in a toast to happiness and friendship. There is a sense of delight and enthusiasm that arises when you are surrounded by the people you hold dear.

Celebrating the good things in life is important, so don't forget to take the time to enjoy them. It's a gentle reminder that it's good to unwind and have a good time every now and then.

However, what's important to note is that the Three of Cups is not solely about partying. It also represents the significance of connection and friendship. Surround yourself with people who lift you up and make you feel good.

When The Three of Cups card appears in a reading, it serves as a gentle reminder to value your friendships and savor the moments of joy that come into your life. Life is a party, get ready to dance!

—Lorelai Hamilton, author of *Teenage Tarot* and
Tarot Tales & Magic Spells

1

The Arcane Room was even more enchanting than I'd imagined. Shelves groaned under the weight of ancient books, crystals caught the light in mesmerizing glints, and the scent of incense wound through the air like a gentle caress. I took a deep breath, trying to ground myself amid the chaos of color and mystery. My fingers skimmed over a deck of tarot cards with the illustration of two women entwined, lips just a whisper apart.

"Interesting choice," a voice murmured from behind me. I turned, and there stood Ms. Vesper, her silver hair cascading in waves down her shoulders, eyes gleaming like she knew every secret I was hiding. She glanced at the deck in my hands, her lips twitching into a wry smile. "Drawn to that one, are you?"

"Couldn't resist," I replied, holding up the deck. "It's got a certain... vibe."

She let out a soft chuckle. "You've got good instincts. That deck is special. Interested in a reading?"

I shrugged, feigning nonchalance though my pulse had quickened. "Why not? I've never had a reading like this before."

Ms. Vesper's eyes twinkled. "Then today's your lucky day."

With a graceful sweep of her hand, she led me to a dimly lit alcove at the back of the store, where the walls were covered in tapestries embroidered with symbols I couldn't quite place. She pulled a deck from a polished wooden box and began to shuffle it, her hands moving with practiced ease. Her rings glinted under the light, a curious mix of silver and moonstone. She laid the deck out in a fan, the cards whispering softly against each other as they spread out before me.

"Pick one," she instructed, her gaze unwavering.

I slid my fingers over the cards, letting them brush against my skin until one practically hummed beneath my touch. When I pulled it from the deck and flipped it over, the Three of Cups stared back at me—three women, laughing, their cups raised high as if in celebration of something unseen.

Ms. Vesper leaned in, her voice low and warm. "The Three of Cups is about connection, friendship... shared joy. But this version has a twist," she said, her gaze shifting back to me. "It hints at boundaries stretched and maybe a little bit more."

"Sounds... interesting," I murmured, barely able to tear my gaze from the card.

Her smile grew, as if she could read the thoughts tumbling through my head. She handed me a steaming cup of tea, the scent of honey and lavender rising to meet me. "Drink this. Then, make yourself comfortable in the room through that door. Let whatever happens, happen."

I moved to the door, finding myself in a small, white-walled room with only a leather chaise lounge in the center. I hesitated but sat down, the cool leather beneath me a stark contrast to the warmth spreading through my body from the tea. Ms. Vesper's eyes met mine one last time before she closed the door with a soft click.

As I sipped, a pleasant heaviness settled over me. My limbs grew warm and heavy, and before I knew it, my eyelids fluttered shut.

When I awoke, the room was silent and still, as if no one had been there at all. Ms. Vesper had vanished, leaving only the faint scent of her perfume lingering in the air. I stood, stretching, and tried to shake off the strange fog clouding my mind. The place was deserted, as if everyone had simply vanished. I called out a quiet, "Thank you," to the empty air and stepped out into the sunlight, breathing in the crisp morning air.

The coffee shop across the street beckoned like a beacon. I needed caffeine, something to jolt me back to reality. The familiar scent of roasting beans wrapped around me as I stepped inside, the quiet hum of conversation and clinking cups grounding me.

As I waited for my order, I felt a pair of eyes on me. Turning, I met the gaze of a woman perched at a nearby table, stirring her coffee lazily. She was striking—short black hair that framed her face in a way that made her cheekbones look like they could cut glass, and eyes so intense they seemed to see right through me.

"Long night?" she asked, a slow smile spreading across her lips.

I raised an eyebrow, trying to match her energy.

"You could say that. And you? What brings you here this morning?"

She leaned forward, resting her chin on her hand, her eyes never leaving mine. "I was just passing through, but I'm glad I stopped. I don't usually meet someone quite as... intriguing."

I laughed, feeling a flush creep up my neck. "Intriguing, huh? That's one way to put it."

She stood up, taking her cup with her, and moved to the counter beside me. "I'm Sam," she said, her voice a rich purr that sent a shiver down my spine.

"Spencer," I replied, my voice a little breathless.

Her gaze dropped to my lips, and then back up to meet my eyes. "Spencer. I like that." Her hand brushed mine as she reached for a napkin, the contact sending sparks up my arm. "You feel like doing something a little... unconventional?"

I arched a brow, intrigued. "I might be up for that."

She nodded toward the back of the shop, where a narrow hallway led to the restrooms. Without a word, she turned and sauntered down the hallway, glancing back once to make sure I was following. My heart pounded as I slipped into the bathroom behind her, locking the door with a soft click.

Before I could catch my breath, her hands were on my waist, pulling me close as her mouth claimed mine. She kissed me like she had something to prove, her lips firm and demanding, her fingers digging into my hips as if she couldn't get enough.

I gasped as she lifted my leg, bracing it on the sink. Her hand slipped beneath the hem of my dress, fingers tracing the curve of my thigh as she pressed me against the wall. Her mouth found my neck, nipping lightly, sending bolts of heat through me.

Her hand slid higher, under my dress, finding the wetness between my folds, and I couldn't help the moan that escaped me. She smiled against my skin, her fingers slipping inside, teasing and coaxing until I was dizzy with need. Her thumb circled my clit, applying just the right amount of pressure, while her other hand pressed gently against my throat, not choking, just holding.

"God, you're so hot," she murmured, her voice a low rasp that made my knees weak. She continued her relentless teasing, each touch sending me higher until the tension finally snapped. I bit down on her shoulder, muffling my cry as the waves of pleasure washed over me.

When it was over, she stepped back, a satisfied

smile playing on her lips. She licked her fingers, savoring the taste with a wink. "Thanks for the morning pick-me-up," she said, smoothing her dress as if nothing had happened.

I leaned against the sink, trying to catch my breath, but she was already gone, leaving me breathless and reeling, wondering how I'd ever explain this to anyone.

2

As I stepped out of the coffee shop, a lingering smile played on my lips, and the morning sun was just starting to warm the sidewalk. I'd barely gone half a block when I heard familiar laughter behind me. I turned, and there they were—Addison and Riley, my best friends since forever, arm in arm, strolling toward me with matching grins.

"Well, well," Riley drawled, her dark eyes twinkling as she took in my flushed cheeks. "Somebody looks like they've been up to no good."

I couldn't help but laugh, feeling that familiar mix of excitement and comfort that always came when they were around. "Let's just say I've had an... interesting morning."

Addison, with her blonde waves and the kind of curves that made you want to give her an appreciative once-over, wrapped an arm around my shoulders, pulling me close. "Sounds like you have a story to tell. But first—how about a sleepover? Just like old times. My place. Tonight."

"A sleepover?" I echoed, feeling a rush of nostalgia hit me. I hadn't had a real slumber party since... well, probably since high school. The idea had a certain pull to it, a kind of magic that only seemed possible when we were all together.

"Exactly like old times," Riley chimed in, slipping her hand into mine. Her fingers wove through mine in a way that felt surprisingly intimate. I looked down, a flutter stirring in my stomach as I remembered how I used to daydream about moments like this, imagining the softness of her skin against mine, our hands intertwined. It felt natural —maybe even too natural.

I squeezed her hand, savoring the warmth of her palm against mine. "I'm in. Let's grab a few things from my place first."

We walked together, Riley's hand still in mine, Addison on my other side, close enough that our shoulders brushed with every step. I felt surrounded, cocooned between them, like we were slipping back into an old rhythm, something we hadn't shared in years.

The walk back to my apartment wasn't long, but they filled it with laughter and little teasing glances that kept my heart racing. Every now and then, I'd catch Addison's gaze lingering on me, a subtle spark in her blue eyes that sent a shiver down my spine. I couldn't tell if I was imagining things or if there was something different in the air today, something charged with possibility.

As we reached my door, Addison leaned against the frame, arms crossed over her chest, giving me an appraising look. "So, tell us about this 'interesting morning' of yours. Don't think we're letting you off that easy."

I fumbled with my keys, grinning at her. "Well, let's just say I met someone in the coffee shop. She was... confident. We might have ended up in the bathroom together."

Addison's eyes widened, and Riley let out a low whistle. "You saucy minx! And here I thought you'd just been catching up on sleep," Riley said, nudging me with her shoulder.

I laughed, shaking my head as I pushed open the door. "It wasn't exactly planned. But she made a move, and, well... I didn't exactly resist."

"Spence, I'm impressed," Addison said, a smirk tugging at the corners of her mouth. She brushed her hand down my arm, her fingers lingering just a moment too long. "You're full of surprises today."

My cheeks flushed as I led them inside, trying not to overthink the way Addison's hand had lingered on my skin. I grabbed a bag from my bedroom and tossed in a few essentials while they hovered around, inspecting the books stacked on my nightstand and teasing me about the state of my closet.

Riley picked up a framed photo of the three of us from our high school days, her smile softening as she traced a finger over the glass. "God, look at us. Feels like another lifetime, doesn't it?"

Addison joined her, the two of them standing so close their arms brushed. "We were such babies back then," she murmured, her voice a little wistful. She looked up, catching my eye. "But some things don't change. I'd still follow you two anywhere."

There was a spark in her gaze that made my pulse skip. I wondered if she felt it too, this crackling tension that seemed to simmer just beneath the surface today. I'd thought about them this way before, of course—little daydreams, fleeting fantasies that I usually brushed off as nothing more than wishful thinking. But here we were, just the three of us, and the air between us felt almost electric.

I shook my head, forcing myself to focus as I zipped up my bag. "Okay, I'm ready. Let's get this slumber party started."

As we headed out, Addison took my bag and slung it over her shoulder, her hand finding the small of my back as we walked. "So, this woman... was she as hot as you?" she asked, her voice teasing.

"Oh, hotter," I replied with a grin, feeling a rush of warmth as she laughed and nudged me.

Riley's fingers brushed mine again, and this time, she slipped her hand back into mine, holding it as if it were the most natural thing in the world. I looked over, and she flashed me a knowing smile, her thumb tracing light circles against my skin. It sent a thrill through me, and I wondered if she could feel my pulse quicken under her touch.

The rest of the walk to Addison's place was filled with their questions, playful and a little prying, and the laughter that bubbled up between us felt like a warm blanket wrapping around my heart. I couldn't help but think back to those high school nights, when we'd pile onto a bed, share secrets in hushed whispers, and promise we'd be friends forever.

Inside, Addison's apartment was cozy and welcoming, with soft lighting and an inviting couch that looked perfect for curling up on. She set my bag down by the door, and Riley kicked off her shoes, making a beeline for the kitchen. "I'll get the wine," she called over her shoulder. "You get the blankets. We're doing this right."

Addison met my gaze, a mischievous glint in her eye. "You heard the lady. Get comfy."

I followed her into the living room, feeling a twinge of excitement as I watched her move, so sure of herself, so at ease. I wondered if they had any idea how many nights I'd spent wishing I could tell them how I really felt, how many times I'd imagined what it would be like to hold their hands, to feel their skin against mine.

The night was just beginning, and with every touch, every glance, I felt the boundaries between us start to blur. I could only hope they were feeling it too.

3

The lights were low, casting a warm glow over Addison's living room as we sprawled across the floor, blankets and pillows piled around us. The air smelled like melted chocolate and the rich, tangy aroma of red wine. I took a sip, savoring the way it lingered on my tongue, and tried to ignore the little thrill that ran through me every time one of them brushed against me.

"So," Addison began, pulling a blanket around her shoulders and nudging Riley with her foot. "What movie are we starting with? I'm in the mood for something fun. Something we haven't seen in a while."

Riley tilted her head, her eyes brightening.

"How about *The Craft*?" She grinned at me, her eyebrow quirking up in that way that always made my heart skip. "Remember when we were obsessed with it?"

I laughed, remembering late nights spent huddled around the TV, wide-eyed as we watched those girls cast spells and cause chaos. "Oh, absolutely. I think we might have all tried levitating each other at least once."

Addison chuckled, raising her glass in a mock toast. "And we failed spectacularly. But I'm down. I haven't seen it in ages." She glanced over at me, her gaze lingering. "Or maybe we go with something more... romantic. Like *10 Things I Hate About You*."

Riley let out a dramatic sigh, rolling her eyes. "Oh god, the number of times you watched that movie." She shot me a mischievous look. "Remember when we were watching it, and you and Addy disappeared for, like, half an hour?"

I felt a blush creep up my cheeks, recalling exactly what had happened. Addison and I had been fourteen, the air heavy with that adolescent mix of nerves and excitement. We'd snuck away under the guise of grabbing snacks, but it hadn't been food we were after.

Addison's laughter was a little softer now, and

she leaned over, brushing a strand of hair from my face. "It was a long time ago, but I remember." She glanced between me and Riley, her smile turning a little sad. "Spence, you ever think about that kiss?"

My heart raced as the memory surfaced—a stolen moment in the dark, her lips on mine, soft and sweet. I'd thought about it more times than I'd ever admit, wondering if it had meant as much to her as it had to me. "You... you remember that?"

She nodded, taking a deep breath. "I remember everything about that night. I also remember pretending it didn't happen the next day, which, looking back, was probably the worst thing I could have done."

Riley, who had been listening quietly, leaned back, watching us with a thoughtful expression. "Why did you pretend it didn't happen, Addy?"

Addison sighed, her gaze dropping to her lap. "I don't know. I was scared, I guess. I'd never kissed a girl before. Didn't know what to do with all those feelings. But, Spence, I've always... I've always had a thing for you." She looked up, meeting my eyes. "I just never thought you felt the same way."

I was stunned. "Addison, are you serious? I had no idea. You never—" I stopped, trying to wrap my mind around it. "You never gave any sign."

She laughed softly, reaching for my hand and threading her fingers through mine. "I guess I didn't know how to. But yeah. I used to lie awake at night, wishing you'd kiss me again."

The weight of her words settled over us, and Riley shifted, clearing her throat. "I think we've all got a story like that. I mean, remember that guy I lost it to during *Scream?*" She rolled her eyes, laughing at herself. "Not my finest moment, but it happened."

Addison grinned, her hand still in mine, and nudged Riley. "How could we forget? You wouldn't shut up about it for weeks. Meanwhile, Spence here wouldn't say a word about anything."

I shrugged, the memories washing over me as I took another sip of wine. "What can I say? I didn't want to jinx it. And besides, that's not exactly first-date material."

Riley laughed, and suddenly I found myself wanting to ask the question that had been sitting in the back of my mind for years. "So... who was everyone's first time?"

Addison's cheeks flushed a little, but she didn't shy away. "Well, for me, it was that boy from the soccer team senior year. Thought he was God's gift to the world, but in hindsight, he had no idea what he was doing." She shook her head, smiling a little. "Guess you could say it was underwhelming."

Riley made a face, nodding in agreement. "Mine was a guy from that band we used to follow around. I don't even remember his name now. But he had a way with words, and I was young and dumb enough to believe every one of them."

I leaned back, listening to their stories, realizing that I'd never really shared mine with them. "Mine was after a night watching *The Notebook*. Romantic as hell, right?" I smirked, thinking back to that moment, the nerves, the clumsy excitement. "But it was awkward. We both thought we knew what we were doing. Spoiler: we didn't. I thought I was never going to find her clit and it was a bit embarrassing."

Addison squeezed my hand, her thumb brushing over my knuckles. "Spence, I wish I'd known. I don't know if I was ever really into those guys. I think I was just looking for something that felt like... well, like this."

The look in her eyes, soft and vulnerable, made my heart ache. I couldn't tell if the wine was making me bold or if it was just years of unsaid words finally bubbling to the surface, but I reached out, tucking a loose strand of hair behind her ear.

"Addy, I've thought about that kiss a hundred times. I always wondered what would have happened if I'd just kissed you again."

Riley leaned over, looping her arm around my shoulders, her voice low. "You still could, you know. We're not fourteen anymore."

Addison laughed, glancing between the two of us. "What are you suggesting, Riley?"

Riley shrugged, her smile a little wicked. "I'm suggesting we stop overthinking it. We've got the wine, the chocolate, the movies... everything we need for a perfect night. Why not see where it takes us?"

The air around us seemed to thrum with tension, each of us caught in the web of old memories and new possibilities. I squeezed Addison's hand, the warmth of Riley's arm around me grounding me as I took a deep breath, feeling like I was standing on the edge of something I'd been waiting for my whole life.

4

The room was quiet except for the soft hum of the movie, the occasional crackle of popcorn, and the gentle clink of our glasses as we sipped wine under the blankets. We'd piled so many around us that it felt like a cocoon, a little fort where only the three of us existed. I was nestled between Addison and Riley, feeling the comforting warmth of their bodies pressing against mine.

Addison had her arm draped casually over my knee, under the blanket, her fingers resting lightly, almost innocently, against my skin. I thought it might have been accidental until I felt her fingers begin to move, tracing slow circles on my knee. The touch was featherlight, barely there, but enough to send a shiver up my spine. I glanced at her out of the corner of my eye, but she was staring at the screen, her expression calm, almost indifferent.

Riley was laughing at something on the screen, her shoulder nudging mine. I forced myself to join in, to keep my reactions under control, even as Addison's fingers continued their slow, teasing exploration up my thigh. I shifted slightly, testing the waters by parting my legs just a little, a silent signal. Her fingers paused, and I held my breath, waiting.

Then, as if she'd been waiting for my permission, her fingers resumed their journey, moving higher, slipping under the edge of my shorts. I sucked in a breath, fighting to keep my face neutral as a wave of heat washed over me. I could feel my pulse quickening, my heart pounding in my chest as her fingers brushed against my inner thigh.

Addison glanced over at me, her lips curving into a sly smile. She leaned in, her breath warm against my ear. "You okay, Spence?" she murmured, her voice low and teasing.

I managed a nod, though my voice was barely more than a whisper. "Yeah... I'm good." I swallowed hard, trying to ignore the way her fingers were tracing patterns on my skin, slow and deliberate.

Riley turned to us, oblivious, a grin on her face. "This scene always cracks me up," she said, pointing to the screen. "Remember that time we tried to reenact it?"

I forced a laugh, nodding along as if my mind wasn't miles away, focused entirely on the subtle movements of Addison's fingers. I could feel my body reacting, a warm ache settling between my legs, my skin tingling where she touched me.

Addison's hand slipped a little further, her fingers grazing the edge of my panties. I held my breath, my entire body taut with anticipation. She met my eyes, her gaze filled with a heat that sent a thrill through me, and then her fingers dipped beneath the fabric, finding my slickness with unerring accuracy. She began to stroke me slowly, each touch sending a fresh surge of pleasure through me.

I fought to keep my breathing steady, to keep my reactions under control, even as my entire body burned with need. I shifted slightly, opening my legs a little wider, giving her better access, and she took full advantage, her fingers slipping inside, her thumb circling my clit in slow, tantalizing strokes.

Riley was still watching the movie, laughing at something on the screen, completely unaware of what was happening right beside her. The thrill of it, the danger of being caught, only heightened the pleasure, making every touch feel that much more intense.

Addison leaned closer, her breath brushing against my neck as her fingers moved faster, driving me higher. "You're so quiet, Spence," she whispered, her voice a warm, teasing caress against my ear. "Trying to be good?"

I bit down on my lip, fighting to keep the moan from escaping. "I... I don't know if I can," I managed, my voice a ragged whisper.

She chuckled softly, her thumb pressing harder against my clit, pushing me closer and closer to the edge. "Just let go," she murmured, her voice a soothing balm against my growing tension. "I've got you."

Her words washed over me, and I surrendered, my body shuddering as the pleasure peaked, a white-hot wave that left me breathless. I stifled my moan with a cough-laugh, hoping Riley wouldn't notice the flush on my cheeks, the way my fingers gripped the blanket as if it were the only thing keeping me grounded.

Addison's fingers lingered, her touch gentle now, tracing lazy circles that sent aftershocks rippling through me. She leaned back, her hand slipping away, leaving me feeling both satisfied and utterly bereft.

Riley turned to us, a playful smile on her face. "You guys are so quiet. Am I missing something?"

Addison shrugged, a mischievous twinkle in her eye as she glanced at me. "Oh, you know us. Just... enjoying the movie."

Riley laughed, tossing a piece of popcorn at Addison, who caught it with ease. "Yeah, sure. Next time, I want in on whatever secret you two are sharing."

Addison winked at me, her smile conspiratorial. "Don't worry, Riley. I'm sure there's plenty more where that came from."

I felt my cheeks flush again, and I took a long sip of wine, hoping to hide the smile tugging at my lips.

5

I slipped away from the cozy cocoon of blankets and laughter, feeling the need to gather myself. The earlier encounter with Addison had left my mind spinning and my body buzzing, so I wandered into the kitchen, hoping that a snack would steady me. I rummaged through the pantry, reaching for a bag of chips on the top shelf, stretching just enough that my skirt lifted, exposing a sliver of skin to the cool air.

That's when I felt her presence.

"Couldn't resist, could you?" Riley's voice was low, her tone teasing as she leaned against the doorway, watching me with a small smile.

I turned to face her, letting the chips drop back into the cabinet. "Just thought I'd grab something while you two finished the movie." My heart was racing again, the way it always did when she was this close, the way she looked at me with that spark in her eyes.

Riley stepped closer, her gaze slipping from my eyes to my mouth, lingering there for a moment before she met my gaze again. "You don't have to pretend, Spence. I can tell something's on your mind."

I bit my lip, trying to hide the blush creeping up my cheeks. "Maybe you're right."

She moved closer, until there was hardly any space between us, her body radiating warmth. Her hands found my hips, pulling me toward her until I was backed up against the counter, my legs pinned between her and the edge. "You sure it's just snacks you're after?" she murmured, her lips brushing mine in the barest hint of a kiss.

I felt a shiver run through me as her lips grazed mine, a touch so light it was almost a tease. "Maybe not," I whispered, my breath mingling with hers. Before I could think, I leaned in, closing the space between us, pressing my lips to hers.

The kiss was slow at first, exploratory, as if we were both testing the waters, but then Riley's hands tightened on my hips, pulling me closer, and I felt a surge of heat rush through me. She kissed me like she'd been waiting her whole life for this moment, her lips firm and demanding, her tongue tracing the edge of my mouth before slipping inside, teasing mine in a way that made my knees weak.

I reached up, wrapping my arms around her shoulders, pulling her closer as she deepened the kiss. Her hands slipped under the hem of my shirt, her fingers tracing the curve of my waist, sending shivers up my spine. I was barely aware of her lifting me onto the counter until I felt the cool surface beneath me, grounding me even as her touch sent me soaring.

Riley stepped between my legs, her hands resting on my thighs, thumbs tracing slow circles that sent a thrill of anticipation through me. I wrapped my legs around her, pulling her closer, feeling the heat of her body pressing against mine. She broke the kiss, trailing her lips down my neck, leaving a path of warmth in her wake.

"You're so beautiful," she murmured against my skin, her voice soft, almost reverent. Her hands wandered, slipping beneath my dress, pushing it up as she kissed her way down my chest, her lips brushing over my collarbone, my skin tingling in the wake of her touch.

I tilted my head back, my breath coming in shallow gasps as her hands moved over me, her touch gentle yet insistent. I felt a strange sense of urgency, a hunger that I hadn't realized I was capable of, and I pulled her closer, needing to feel her, to have her as close as possible.

Her gaze dropped to the counter beside me, and she picked up a cucumber with a playful grin. "You know," she said, holding it up between us, "I've always wondered..."

I let out a breathless laugh, my cheeks flushing with anticipation as I nodded, giving her permission. She moved back, her gaze never leaving mine as she slowly slid the cucumber between my legs, pressing it against my hot, wet, center, testing my reaction.

The coolness of it sent a shock through me, and I gasped, my fingers gripping the edge of the counter as she began to move, her touch gentle yet firm. She watched me closely, her eyes filled with a mixture of curiosity and desire as she pushed it deeper, her movements slow and deliberate, drawing out every reaction, every shiver and moan.

I felt my body tense, the pleasure building in slow, relentless waves, each movement of her hand bringing me closer to the edge. My breath was coming in short gasps, my body on fire as she worked me, her eyes dark with intensity as she watched me fall apart beneath her touch.

Riley leaned in, her lips brushing mine as she whispered, "You're so responsive, Spence. I could watch you like this forever."

Her words sent a fresh surge of heat through me, and I felt myself tipping over the edge, my body shuddering as the pleasure peaked, a wave of ecstasy washing over me that left me breathless and trembling. I clung to her, my nails digging into her shoulders as I rode out the high, feeling like I was floating, lost in a sea of sensation.

When I finally came back to earth, Riley was there, steadying me, her hands gentle as she lowered me back onto the counter. She knelt between my legs, her mouth finding my center, tasting me with a reverence that made my heart ache. Her tongue was soft, gentle, drawing out the last shudders of pleasure as she held me close, her hands gripping my thighs as if she couldn't bear to let me go.

I leaned back, my head resting against the cabinet, my body spent and sated, feeling like I'd just been through something transformative, something that had changed me in ways I couldn't quite understand. Riley stood, her gaze meeting mine with a satisfied smile, and she leaned in, pressing a gentle kiss to my lips.

"I've wanted to do that for so long," she murmured, her fingers brushing a stray strand of hair from my face.

I reached up, pulling her close, my heart swelling with a mix of gratitude and desire. "Me too," I whispered, my voice barely more than a breath, but she heard me, and her smile widened, her eyes bright with joy.

6

I woke to the smell of bacon and the sound of laughter drifting down the hall. Sunlight streamed through the window, warming the room as I blinked the sleep from my eyes. The memories of the night before flooded back in a wave, and I couldn't help the smile that crept across my face as I rolled out of bed, slipping on a shirt before heading toward the kitchen.

As I reached the doorway, I paused, taking in the scene. Riley and Addison were dancing around the kitchen, spatulas in hand, the music turned up as they twirled and laughed, flipping pancakes and stirring eggs. I watched them for a moment, a sense of warmth filling my chest. This was home. This was where I belonged.

Addison spotted me first, breaking into a grin. "Look who decided to join us!" she called, flipping a pancake with an exaggerated flourish.

"Morning, sleepyhead!" Riley added, nudging me with her hip as I joined them at the counter. "We're making the ultimate breakfast feast. Pancakes, bacon, eggs... the works."

I laughed, grabbing a knife and a bowl of fresh strawberries from the fridge. "Guess I'll be on fruit duty, then," I said, starting to slice the strawberries as I fell into the familiar rhythm of our friendship.

They continued to dance around the kitchen as they cooked, adding scrambled eggs and sausage to the growing pile of food on the counter. I cut up strawberries, pineapple, and melon, the scents mingling in a heady mix that made my stomach rumble with anticipation.

We carried everything over to the table, loading up our plates with pancakes smothered in syrup, crispy bacon, and fresh fruit. As we settled in, Addison glanced over at me, her eyes sparkling with mischief. "Do you remember when we used to have those 'Newsies' parties?"

I couldn't help but laugh, nodding as the memories washed over me. "Oh my gods, yes. We watched that movie every weekend for, what, five years straight?"

Riley groaned, rolling her eyes. "I'm pretty sure we could still recite every line if we tried. We were obsessed."

"Newsies every Friday and Saturday night," Addison chimed in, grinning. "We'd quote the lines, dance around the room... I think we even tried to learn the choreography at one point."

"Of course we did," I replied, chuckling as I remembered our high school selves, giddy with excitement as we watched the same scenes over and over, staying up until the early hours of the morning. "We must've driven our parents crazy."

Riley smirked, raising her glass of orange juice in a mock toast. "To our poor, long-suffering parents. They put up with a lot."

We clinked glasses, laughing as we reminisced, the years melting away as we recounted the silly things we'd done together—sleepovers that stretched into whole weekends, midnight snack runs, and the time we'd stayed up until dawn trying to catch the sunrise, only to fall asleep minutes before it happened.

As we finished breakfast, Addison glanced over

at me, a playful glint in her eyes. "You know, there's one thing we haven't done in a while."

I raised an eyebrow, grinning. "Oh? And what's that?"

"Truth or dare," she replied, a mischievous smile spreading across her face. "Come on, it's been forever since we played. And after last night... I think it could get interesting."

I glanced at Riley, who was already nodding, a similar sparkle in her eyes. "I'm game," she said, her voice laced with anticipation.

I shrugged, leaning back in my chair. "Alright, I'm in. Who's going first?"

Addison sat up straighter, looking between the two of us. "I'll go first. Spencer—truth or dare?"

I hesitated for a moment, then decided to start simple. "Truth."

She leaned in, her gaze piercing as she asked, "What's the one sexual fantasy you've always wanted to try but never have?"

I felt a blush creeping up my neck, but I met her gaze, the playful energy between us emboldening me. "I've always wanted to try... public sex. Like, somewhere risky, where we could get caught." I took a breath, feeling a thrill rush through me as I confessed, but Addison and Riley only exchanged glances, their eyes lighting up with shared excitement.

Riley grinned, clearly enjoying my answer. "Interesting... we'll have to keep that in mind." She winked at me, sending a shiver through my spine. Then she turned to Addison. "Alright, Addy—truth or dare?"

Addison grinned, her eyes narrowing. "Dare. Let's make it interesting."

Riley thought for a moment, a slow smile spreading across her face. "I dare you to... kiss Spencer. Like you mean it."

Addison didn't hesitate. She leaned over, cupping my face with one hand as she brought her lips to mine. The kiss was slow and sensual, deepening as her hand slid to the back of my neck, pulling me closer. I could feel my heart racing as her tongue teased mine, her lips soft but insistent, leaving me breathless by the time she pulled away.

I opened my eyes to find Riley watching us, her expression hungry as she licked her lips. "Wow," she murmured, her voice barely more than a whisper. "That was... something."

Addison smirked, wiping her thumb over my bottom lip. "Your turn, Spence. Truth or dare?"

My pulse was still racing from the kiss, and I felt a surge of courage. "Dare."

She glanced at Riley, a wicked grin spreading across her face. "I dare you to give Riley a lap dance."

Riley raised an eyebrow, looking more than a little intrigued. "Well, I'm not going to say no to that."

Laughing, I stood up, taking Riley's hand and pulling her onto the couch. The music played softly in the background as I straddled her lap, moving my hips in time with the beat, feeling her hands settle on my waist. Her eyes were dark with desire as I leaned in, trailing my hands over her shoulders, arching my back as I moved against her, every touch, every look between us charged with an electricity that left me breathless.

When I finally pulled away, I sat back down, my skin flushed, my body humming with anticipation. Riley took a deep breath, looking at me like she was trying to memorize every inch of me.

Addison broke the silence, grinning as she leaned back. "Riley, truth or dare?"

"Truth," she replied, her gaze never leaving mine.

Addison leaned forward, her voice low. "What's

the most intimate thing you've ever wanted to do with one of us?"

Riley hesitated, glancing between us before she spoke, her voice barely more than a whisper. "I've always wanted to... tie Spencer up. Explore her body. Take my time."

My breath caught, and I felt a surge of heat rush through me, a potent mixture of excitement and longing that seemed to pulse between us. This game—what had started as playful dares and teasing questions—was stripping away the last remnants of distance, exposing all the emotions that we had once kept safely hidden. Every truth revealed, every touch shared, seemed to dissolve another barrier until there was nothing left between us but raw, honest vulnerability. I looked at them both, feeling their presence like a tangible warmth, the love and desire in their eyes mirroring my own.

Addison's fingers intertwined with mine, her grip firm and reassuring, while Riley reached over to tuck a strand of hair behind my ear, her touch lingering. In that moment, I realized just how deeply connected we were, how much we had always been, even if we had never dared to fully admit it. We were bound by years of memories, laughter, and shared secrets, and now, finally, by the unspoken emotions that had hovered between us for so long. It felt like all the pieces were finally falling into place, and I could barely breathe from the intensity of it.

We continued the game, each question and each dare drawing us closer, the boundaries between friendship and something more blurring beyond recognition. I could feel the walls around my heart softening, dissolving with every whispered confession and lingering touch. Addison and Riley looked at me with an openness that was both thrilling and terrifying, their eyes filled with promises and possibilities.

By the time we finished, we were tangled together on the couch, our bodies draped over one another like we were trying to merge into a single being. The room was filled with the sound of our quiet laughter, the echoes of our confessions hanging in the air like a gentle reminder of all we'd shared. The first light of morning filtered through the window, casting a soft glow over us, and I felt cocooned in the warmth of their presence, surrounded by a love that was deep, abiding, and impossibly tender.

As I lay there between them, basking in the afterglow of our game, I realized that this was what it meant to truly come home. It wasn't just the memories or the laughter or the familiar touch—it was the way they saw me, completely, and still wanted to stay. I closed my eyes, letting the feeling wash over me, knowing that no matter what came next, I would always have this. I would always have them.

7

After breakfast, the three of us collapsed back onto the couch, feeling sated and content, and decided to put on another movie. We ended up playing rock-paper-scissors to see who'd be the unlucky one to leave our cozy nest and pick up lunch. Luck wasn't on my side this time.

"Alright, alright," I groaned, slipping into my shoes. "I'll go grab us some food. You two better not finish this movie without me!"

They waved me off with matching grins, and I made my way out the door, stepping into the warmth of the midday sun. The town was quiet, a gentle breeze rustling through the trees as I strolled down the familiar streets. On a whim, I decided to stop by Spellbound Stories. I'd been meaning to grab a particular book for a while now, and I figured it was as good a time as any.

The bell above the door chimed as I stepped inside, inhaling the comforting scent of books and a hint of lavender from the candles burning on the counter. I scanned the aisles, my eyes landing on Lea, the store's owner, who was busy rearranging a shelf of hardcovers. She looked up as I approached, a warm smile lighting up her face.

"Spencer! It's been a while," she greeted, brushing a strand of red hair behind her ear. Lea was striking—tall and effortlessly sexy, with a confidence that had always intrigued me. Her gaze lingered on me, and I felt a familiar thrill run through me.

"It has," I replied, stepping closer. "I've missed stopping by. You look as gorgeous as ever, Lea."

Her smile widened, and she arched an eyebrow. "Well, aren't you sweet? What brings you in today?"

I leaned against the shelf, meeting her gaze with a grin. "I came for a book, but now that I'm here... I'm thinking I'd rather have my way with you between the shelves."

Her eyes sparkled with mischief, and she took a step closer, closing the distance between us. "Is that so?" she murmured, her voice a low purr that made my pulse quicken.

Before I could respond, the door chimed again, and I turned to see Alex, Lea's husband, striding into the store. He was ruggedly handsome, with an easy charm and a smile that seemed to always be at the ready. He walked over to Lea, pressing a kiss to her cheek before turning to me with a grin.

"Spencer! Good to see you. Which book has got you stopping by?"

Lea shot me a sly glance before turning to Alex. "Spencer here is looking for a new experience," she said, her tone laced with innuendo as she winked at him.

Alex's grin widened, and he raised an eyebrow. "Oh? What kind of experience are we talking about?"

Lea leaned in, whispering something in his ear that I couldn't quite catch, but whatever she said made him chuckle, his eyes gleaming with excitement. He looked back at me, his gaze appraising. "Well, now... that does sound interesting."

I felt a blush creep up my cheeks, realizing the

situation I'd walked myself into. "Oh, I was just... I mean, I didn't mean to—"

Lea cut me off with a laugh, placing a hand on my arm. "Spence, don't backpedal now. You've piqued my interest." She glanced over at Alex, sharing a silent conversation, their expressions speaking volumes. "What do you say, love? Should we give her a little adventure?"

Alex grinned, nodding. "I think we should. But only if I get to watch."

My heart skipped a beat, and I felt a rush of excitement. "You mean... really?"

Lea moved closer, her eyes locking onto mine. "Absolutely. I've always wanted to do this," she murmured, taking my hand and leading me toward the back of the store, where the aisles were hidden from view. Alex followed, his gaze steady and filled with anticipation.

Once we were tucked away in a secluded corner, Lea leaned against the shelf, pulling me toward her. "Someone could walk in at any moment," she whispered, her voice filled with a delicious tension. "Doesn't that turn you on, Spence?"

I bit my lip, nodding as I felt the familiar thrill of excitement surge through me. "You have no idea," I replied, my voice barely more than a breath.

She closed the distance between us, pressing her lips to mine with a hunger that made my knees weak. I wrapped my arms around her, pulling her close as our kiss deepened, my hands exploring the curve of her waist, the warmth of her skin beneath her shirt. Her body pressed against mine, pinning me to the shelf as we lost ourselves in the kiss, our breaths mingling, our hearts racing.

Lea broke away, her lips trailing down my neck, her hands slipping under my shirt as she pulled it up, exposing my skin to the cool air. I shivered as she leaned down, taking one of my breasts into her mouth, her tongue tracing circles around my nipple, making it harden beneath her touch. I gasped, gripping the edge of the shelf as she continued her exploration, her mouth leaving a trail of heat in its wake.

Out of the corner of my eye, I saw Alex watching us, his eyes dark with desire, his lips parted as he took in every detail. I met his gaze, feeling a new surge of excitement at the way he watched, his expression a mix of admiration and longing.

Lea's hands moved lower, finding the waistband of my skirt, and she glanced up at me, her eyes filled with a question. I nodded, giving her permission, and she slipped her hand beneath the fabric, her fingers finding my center, already wet with anticipation. She began to move, her touch gentle but insistent, sending waves of pleasure through me as she worked me with practiced skill.

I closed my eyes, letting the sensation wash over me, feeling my body respond to her every touch, every movement. I could hear Alex's breath quicken, and the sound only heightened the experience, adding a new layer of excitement to the already charged atmosphere.

Lea's fingers moved faster, her other hand gripping my hip as she brought me closer and closer to the edge. I could feel the tension building, my body tightening as I hovered on the brink, and then, with a final push, I came, a shuddering wave of pleasure that left me breathless and trembling in her arms.

As I came down from the high, I felt Lea's lips on mine once more, soft and gentle, a contrast to the intensity of our encounter. Alex moved closer, pressing a kiss to Lea's cheek, his hand resting on her shoulder as he looked at me with a satisfied smile.

"Lea's been wanting to do that for a while now,"

he murmured, his voice filled with warmth. "This was my gift to her."

I smiled, feeling a deep sense of gratitude and connection as I took in the two of them, standing there together, their love for each other as clear as the desire we'd just shared. In that moment, I felt like I'd found something rare and beautiful.

8

As I left Spellbound Stories, a smile played on my lips, and I felt a surge of confidence. My body still hummed with the remnants of my encounter with Lea and Alex, and my mind replayed every delicious moment. I felt alive, like a version of myself I'd always wanted to be but had only just discovered. The sun was bright overhead, and the world seemed to pulse with energy, as if I'd been given some secret that only I could understand.

I continued down the street, my stride easy, savoring the way people glanced my way, almost as if they could sense the change in me. I was drawn to the bright red sign of Golden Chopsticks, the smell of stir-fried vegetables and spices drifting out as I reached for the door.

But as soon as my hand touched the door handle, the world spun around me, and suddenly, I wasn't standing on the street anymore. I was back in the Arcane Room, lying on the chaise lounge, blinking up at the ceiling as if I'd just woken from a dream.

"Ah, you're back," came Ms. Vesper's familiar voice, warm and steady. She was seated at the foot of the couch, her legs crossed, watching me with a knowing smile. "How are you feeling?"

I sat up slowly, glancing around the room, my heart pounding as I tried to make sense of it. "Wait... so it was all...?"

She nodded, her smile widening. "Yes. Everything you experienced was part of the journey brought on by the tea and the Three of Cups."

I took a deep breath, the memories flooding back with an almost overwhelming intensity. "It felt so real," I murmured, running a hand through my hair. "The night with my friends, the coffee shop, the bookstore... every single moment felt real."

Ms. Vesper leaned forward, her gaze kind. "That's the magic of the Arcane Room. It brings out the desires, the emotions you carry with you, and helps you explore them in a way that feels tangible and safe. You experienced what you needed to experience."

I met her eyes, a wave of gratitude washing over me. "It's like... I feel more myself than I ever have. Like I've uncovered something I didn't even know was missing."

Ms. Vesper nodded, her smile gentle. "The Three of Cups is about connection, celebration, and self-discovery. You've always had that strength within you, Spencer. This journey simply allowed you to see it, to embody it, without the weight of everyday life holding you back."

I took a moment to reflect on her words, letting them sink in. Everything I'd felt over the course of that night—the love, the desire, the freedom—had left an indelible mark on me. I'd always known I cared deeply for Addison and Riley, but now I saw our connection with new clarity. And the experiences with the women I'd encountered along the way had shown me a new side of myself, one that was confident and unafraid to embrace what she wanted.

"I feel... liberated," I said, the words surprising me even as I spoke them. "Like I'm not afraid anymore. I'm ready to go after what I want, to be who I want to be."

Ms. Vesper's eyes twinkled with approval. "That's exactly what I hoped you would find. The Arcane Room offers the path, but you walk it."

I took a deep breath, feeling a sense of fulfillment that resonated deeply within me. "Thank you," I murmured, the words filled with a quiet gratitude. "I don't think I'll ever look at life the same way again."

Ms. Vesper stood, moving to the door, her movements graceful and fluid. "Remember, Spencer, the magic of the Three of Cups is with you, even outside the Arcane Room. You carry it with you in every connection you make, in every truth you embrace. It's not something you leave behind."

As I stood to join her, I felt a weight lift from my shoulders, a sense of lightness that I hadn't realized I'd been missing. I turned to face her, feeling the warmth of her presence and the wisdom she'd shared. "I'll hold onto that," I promised, a smile tugging at the corners of my lips. "It's time I started living the way I always dreamed I could."

With a nod, Ms. Vesper opened the door, and I stepped out into the world again, feeling as if I was seeing it for the first time. The town looked the same, but I knew that I'd changed. I'd been given a glimpse of my deepest desires, my truest self, and I wasn't about to let that go.

I'd found my way home to myself, and there was nothing that could take that away from me.

SIGN up for Jax Wilder's newsletter and receive a collection of unpublished Coral Cove short stories. Meet familiar characters and dive deeper into the love and romance that Coral Cove is known for. Don't miss out on this exclusive content!

https://mailchi.mp/158597581671/jax-wilder

If you enjoyed the *3 of Cups*, I hope you'll

check out **_Dawning Desire_** in my Coral Cove series.

SAPPHIC LOVE, divine desire, cosmic passion.

LILLY

I was betrothed.

I was never supposed to fall in love with beauty as radiant as the moonlight itself.

But we fell in love anyway.

The gods cursed my love to live as a human for ten-thousand years.

She forgets who I am over and over and over.

So, I have to reminder her.

OPHELIA

She took my books.

Then she took my breath.

I can't shake the feeling that I've known her before.

Maybe in another life.

But I don't have time for love while I'm trying to make partner.

. . .

Cosmic love, destined passion, irresistible desire.

Tai-Yang, goddess of the sun, has always followed the celestial laws. Destined to be with Hou Yi, the famed archer of the skies, her fate seemed certain—until she met Luna, the goddess of the moon. Their forbidden connection burned brighter than the stars, and in their love, Tai-Yang found something worth defying the gods for.

But love between goddesses comes with consequences. Banished to Earth and reincarnated over centuries, Luna forgets Tai-Yang with every new life. Yet during a rare eclipse, memories return for a fleeting moment, reigniting the passion and love between them. Will they break the gods' curse or face eternal separation?

Dawning Desire is a heart-pounding FF romance that blends mythological elements, forbidden love, and cosmic passion. Perfect for fans of sapphic romance and powerful goddesses defying destiny.

Jax Wilder

3 of Swords

Three
of Swords

Tarot Fantasies Series

THREE OF SWORDS

Tarot Temptations Series

3 OF SWORDS

"This too shall pass," 3 of Swords.

Key Words and Phrases
Heartbreak, breakup, and sorrow
Emotional pain and grief
Betrayal and loss
Disappointment and sadness
Painful truths and revelations
Healing and forgiveness
Letting go of pain from the past
Emotional release and catharsis
Moving forward with resilience and strength

The Three of Swords can be tough to see because it's about heartbreak and sadness. Imagine feeling like three sharp swords pierced your heart, causing pain and sorrow. It represents heartbreak and emotional pain. It's okay to feel hurt and upset. Sometimes life throws us curveballs, and it's important to acknowledge our emotions. Give yourself permission to grieve and process the pain you're feeling.

This pain won't last forever, you will heal. You have the strength within you to overcome and emerge stronger on the other side. Let go of what no longer serves you. Holding onto resentment or anger will only weigh you down. It's time to release those negative emotions and make room for healing and growth.

—Lorelai Hamilton, author of *Teenage Tarot* and *Tarot Tales & Magic Spells*

1

"Take your time, dear. I'll be just a few moments," the tattooed woman said as she led my best friend of fifteen years into the back room.

I nodded and decided to explore the store. The Arcane Room had been gaining a reputation as a place where one could have a unique experience. I had my doubts, especially since Bethany, a notorious exaggerator, had been the one to recommend it. Still, I'd do anything for my best friend Andrew, to help him find the confidence he needed to start dating again. Lately, I'd even begun to wonder if he was interested in men at all.

The Arcane Room was unlike any store I'd ever seen. It had a mystical ambiance, pulsing with an energy that seemed to have a life of its own. The air was thick with the subtle scent of incense—sandalwood, mixed with something floral I couldn't quite place. Soft, music played in the background, creating a calming atmosphere that chipped away at my initial skepticism.

In the center of the room, was the center piece a torso sized piece of rich purple amethyst. Just to the right was a waist-high glass display case held hundreds of small glass bowls filled with an array of crystals, rocks, and minerals—the largest assortment I'd ever seen. Each bowl had a small label indicating the name and purported properties of its contents: amethyst for protection, rose quartz for love, citrine for prosperity. The colors were vibrant, each stone catching the light as if it were alive.

Shelves lined the walls, filled with items that looked both ancient and mystical. Rows of tarot card decks with beautifully illustrated covers, books on astrology and spellcasting, candles in every color and scent imaginable, jars of herbs, and small vials of essential oils were all meticulously arranged. The combination of scents was overwhelming, making me feel slightly lightheaded but oddly at peace.

Delicate wind chimes and dream catchers hung from the ceiling, their gentle movements creating a soft, tinkling sound that added to the store's enchanting vibe. In one corner, a table was set up for tarot readings. Andrew had just chosen his card, though I hadn't seen which one. Curious, I wandered over to the table for a sneak peek.

The table was covered with a rich, dark velvet cloth, adorned with a crystal ball, candles, and various other items I couldn't identify. It looked like the shopkeeper had already reshuffled the deck, so Andrew's card would remain a mystery until he shared it on the ride home.

A flicker of light caught my attention, and I turned to see a collection of beautifully crafted jewelry: amulets, rings, and necklaces designed to harness the power of the stones they held. Each piece looked unique, as if it had its own story. A small sign indicated these were made by local artists. I always appreciate when shops support local talent.

Despite my initial doubts, I could see why The Arcane Room was gaining popularity. There was something special about this place, a sense of mystery and possibility that was hard to ignore. Maybe Bethany's stories weren't all exaggerations after all.

"Now, what can I do for you, dear?" a voice behind me rang out like a bell.

I jumped.

"Oh, I'm sorry, dear, I thought you heard me coming," she laughed.

"My goodness, no! I didn't mean to be so startled. I was just so taken with these beautiful pieces," I said, trying to calm my racing heart.

The woman gave me a kind, knowing smile. "Everything on the upper shelf was made by my dear friend Melinda. She can't make them anymore due to her arthritis, so what you see is all we'll ever have."

"Oh no, that's too bad. It's beautiful work," I said.

"I'm Ms. Vesper, by the way," she held out her hand, palm down.

I took her fingers and gave a gentle shake. "I'm Larissa."

"That's a lovely name," she said. "A beautiful name for a beautiful woman."

"Thank you," I replied, a little flustered. "Ms. Vesper is a unique name as well."

"Unique name for a unique lady," she chuckled, her laugh more of a cackle, sending a shiver down my spine. Ms. Vesper had an odd charm—warm and friendly, yet there was an air of mystery about her, a subtle hint of danger that lingered in her presence. "So, my dear, what brings you to The Arcane Room?"

"Oh, my friend Andrew, the one you took to the back," I pointed to the door he had gone through. "He's been awfully pent up for years. I heard this was the place to help him with his…apprehension. We drove up to Coral Cove this morning."

Ms. Vesper paused, looking me up and down. "I know all about young Andrew. But what about you, my dear? What is it that you need?"

"Me? I'm good," I laughed nervously. "I have a great life. A wonderful therapist. I love my job. I have a fantastic boyfriend. Zero complaints."

Ms. Vesper studied me again before grabbing both of my hands, holding them just above my waist as she stared into my eyes. "Come with me, my dear. Let's draw you a card."

"Oh, I couldn't possibly," I said, trying to pull my hands back. She held onto my right hand and led me to her table.

"Let's just take a look, shall we?" Ms. Vesper said. "No pressure."

I stifled a small laugh. No pressure? The woman had a death grip on my hand and was practically dragging me to the table. She placed me in front of it, then moved to the other side. She shuffled the deck a few times before fanning out the cards in front of me.

"Choose one," she said.

"No. I don't need to. This is for Andrew," I said as politely as possible.

"Andrew will be done soon," she said. "You'll have plenty of time for your own turn."

"I only came here for Andrew," I protested again. "I didn't bring enough money for my own experience."

"Money is no issue here, my dear. Your first experience is complimentary, just like Andrew's. My treat," she said.

"Really?"

"Yes. I love to help people. I know it sounds too good to be true, but seriously, you must need to be here, or the magic of Coral Cove wouldn't have brought you," she said. "Plus, if you feel I deserve a gratuity afterward, you're more than welcome to do so."

Ms. Vesper gave a coy wink, acknowledging the humor in her own words. Realizing it was futile to resist, I reached out and selected a card near the front of the deck. I flipped it over and showed it to Ms. Vesper.

"The Three of Swords," she said. "Very interesting."

"What? What does it mean?" I asked. I'd had my tarot cards read before, but I didn't have each card memorized.

"It means you were brought here for an experience," Ms. Vesper said. "The Three of Swords often signifies grief, suffering, and loss. But there is strength in it as well—strength in expression, transformation, and cleansing. This is a very good card for you, I think."

A small buzzer went off behind Ms. Vesper, and she turned to disappear for a few minutes. I stared at the card in front of me—the bright red heart pierced by three swords, bleeding down to the bottom of the card. What possible good could come from such a negative-sounding card?

A moment later, Andrew emerged from the back room with Ms. Vesper, his face flushed. He couldn't make eye contact with me.

"Good experience?" I asked, teasingly.

Andrew just nodded, still avoiding my gaze.

"Geez, I don't think I've ever seen you so speechless," I laughed. "Shall we get going then?"

Andrew finally met my eyes, his tone serious but gentle. "No, you have to try that…"

"Come, dear, I've just finished your tea," Ms. Vesper said as she walked back into the room. I glanced at Andrew, who simply nodded. My heart began to race as I followed Ms. Vesper.

The room she led me to wasn't large, but it was stark white—a sharp contrast to the rest of the shop, devoid of decoration. In the middle of the room was a single black leather chaise lounge.

"Sit, my dear, make yourself comfortable," Ms. Vesper said as she handed me a cup of tea. "This is for the experience. Don't worry about the time— you'll only be in the experience for twenty minutes, just like Andrew."

I took a sip of the tea, surprised by its drinkable temperature.

"Drink, drink," Ms. Vesper encouraged. I did as I was told, and the room began to slip away.

"Larissa," I managed to reply, grabbing his hand. His skin was smooth, and I wondered if he had ever worked a day in his life.

"Hello, Larissa," he said, a smile tugging at the corners of his mouth. "What brings you to this part of town?"

I swallowed hard, glancing around nervously. "I'm not even sure how I got here."

"Where were you trying to go?" he asked, his smile widening.

I hesitated for a moment, not even sure myself of what was happening. I had been in Coral Cove, and it was midday. Now, it appeared I was in New York City or Chicago, and it was dark. I looked around, trying to come up with some sort of answer.

Sensing my hesitation, Vlad placed a gentle hand on my shoulder. "Come. Let's get you out of this alleyway at least."

Vlad guided me down the alley and out to a main street. The bright lights of the city made me feel safer than I had in the dingy alley. The buildings towered overhead like beacons as far as I could see in either direction. Yet, I still couldn't make out what city I was in.

"Where are we?" I asked.

"Midtown," Vlad answered. I really meant what city we were in but decided not to clarify my question. Being alone in a big city as a woman was enough to make me uneasy. I wasn't going to admit that I had no clue where I was.

As we walked, I glanced at Vlad from the corner of my eye. He moved with an effortless grace, his presence commanding attention even amidst the bustling crowd. There was a mystery about him that drew me in, and I couldn't help but feel a spark of attraction.

We passed by a food cart, the smell of sizzling meat and spices wafting through the air. My stomach growled, and Vlad seemed to notice.

"Hungry?" he asked with a charming smile.

"Starving," I admitted, my cheeks flushing.

"Let's get you something to eat, then," he said, steering me toward the cart.

Vlad ordered for me, his voice smooth and confident as he spoke to the vendor. A few moments later, he handed me a hot sandwich wrapped in foil. The warmth seeped into my cold hands, and I took a grateful bite. The flavors exploded in my mouth, and I couldn't help but let out a small moan of satisfaction.

"Good?" Vlad asked, amusement playing on his face.

"Delicious," I replied. "How much do I owe you?"

"It's on me," he smiled.

"You're not getting anything?" I asked.

"I just finished dinner right before I found you in the alley."

We continued to walk, the sounds of the city creating a strange symphony around us. Vlad pointed out various landmarks, sharing little anecdotes about each one. I still couldn't decipher what city we were in, but I found myself relaxing in Vlad's presence and caring less about the details.

"So, Vlad," I said between bites, "what do you do?"

He chuckled softly. "I suppose you could say I'm an investor. I have a knack for seeing potential where others might not."

"As long as you enjoy what you do, I guess," I teased, feeling a bit bolder.

He smiled, a softness beginning to shine through. "And what about you, Larissa? What do you do?"

"I'm an ultrasound technician," I said confidently.

"For babies?" His face lit up with an adorable, childlike expression.

"Yes. That's my specialty. You can get an ultrasound for all sorts of ailments, but I work at a fertility clinic, so I get to look at babies all day," I said.

His eyes sparkled. "That's amazing. It must be very fulfilling."

"Thank you for saying that. Yes, I love my job." I really did. His words and excitement about my job struck a chord within me, and I found myself smiling and nodding like an idiot. There was something about Vlad that made me feel seen, understood in a way I hadn't felt in a long time.

As we continued to stroll through the city, our conversation flowed effortlessly. Vlad was attentive, genuinely interested in what I had to say. The initial fear I felt had long faded, replaced by a growing curiosity and undeniable attraction.

Jason, my boyfriend, had never shown this much interest in my life. I thought that was just how straight men were. Andrew cared about my job and my life. That's probably why I went to him with everything instead of Jason. Wasn't that just the way it is?

Eventually, we found ourselves in a quieter part

of the city, the noise and lights dimming around us. Vlad led me to a small park, the trees casting long shadows under the streetlights. We sat on a bench, the cool night air wrapping around us.

"Thank you for tonight," I said softly, looking up at him. "I don't know what I would have done if you hadn't found me."

"It was my pleasure, Larissa," he replied, his voice low and soothing. "I'm glad we crossed paths."

Our eyes locked, the electricity between us palpable. For a moment, it felt as if the entire world had fallen away, leaving just the two of us in this quiet corner of the city.

"I really want to kiss you," Vlad said.

3

Instinctively, I reached up, grabbed Vlad by the back of the head, and pulled him toward me. Our lips met, and fireworks exploded inside me. His lips were soft yet demanding, moving against mine with a passion that took my breath away. I melted into the kiss, my body pressing closer as if drawn by an irresistible force.

Vlad's hands found their way to my waist, pulling me tighter against him. The heat between us rose, a slow burn that ignited every nerve ending in my body. His tongue traced the seam of my lips, and I parted them eagerly, allowing him deeper access. The taste of him was intoxicating—sweet with an edge of danger that sent shivers through my body.

His fingers tangled in my hair, gently tugging me closer as our kiss deepened. My hands roamed over his shoulders, feeling the hard muscles beneath his shirt. He groaned deeply into my mouth, the sound vibrating through me, fueling the fire already burning within.

I broke the kiss just long enough to gasp for air and looked into Vlad's eyes. They were dark, filled with an intensity that made my heart race even faster.

"Fuck. Jason."

Before I could protest, he captured my lips again, his kiss more urgent this time. His hands roamed over my back, tracing every curve and dip, making me ache for more of his touch.

Sensing my unease, he paused. "Everything okay?"

"Yes, I just…" I thought about The Arcane Room, about Andrew's face, flushed with satisfaction. This isn't real. I'm not cheating. I'm having an experience. I decided to forget Jason and accept this. I looked up and down at the sexy man in front of me. "We just met. I feel a little awkward, I guess."

Vlad smiled. "You seemed to be enjoying yourself a minute ago. It couldn't have been too awkward."

"Very true," I nodded, and pounced into his lap. The world around us faded away, leaving just the two of us lost in the moment. Every kiss, every touch, felt like a promise of more to come—a tantalizing preview of the passion ahead.

Vlad broke the kiss again. He grabbed the back of my head, his grip gentle but strong. "You are the most beautiful woman I've ever met."

I felt my cheeks flush. "Thank you."

"I want to show you something," Vlad said, standing up and taking my hand. We left the park and started toward a different part of the city.

With our hands entwined, he led me through the bustling streets. The noise and chaos of the city blurred into the background as we turned down a narrow side street, then another, until we reached an old, abandoned warehouse. Its dilapidated exterior seemed out of place among the modern buildings, but something about it intrigued me.

Vlad pushed open a rusty door and guided me inside. The interior was dark and empty, with the faint sound of footsteps echoing in the vast space. He led me to a side door, and we entered a more modern, well-lit lobby. Vlad's presence was reassuring, his confidence infectious. He led me into an elevator and pressed the top button.

When we reached the top, Vlad pushed open a door that led to the roof. I stepped into the cool night air and gasped. The city sprawled out before us—a sea of twinkling lights and towering skyscrapers. But what truly took my breath away was the sky. Above us, the stars shone brightly, more vivid and numerous than I ever expected to see in the city.

"This is the only place in town where you can see the stars like this," Vlad said softly, his voice a mix of pride and tenderness. "I wanted to share it with you."

We walked to the edge of the roof, and Vlad wrapped his arm around my shoulders, pulling me close. The warmth of his body against mine was comforting, and I leaned into him, feeling a sense of peace wash over me.

"Thank you," I whispered, my voice barely audible over the gentle breeze. "It's beautiful."

We stood there, wrapped in each other's embrace, the stars our only witnesses. Vlad's hand traced slow, soothing patterns on my back, and my heart swelled with emotions I couldn't quite name. This man, this night, felt like a dream, one I never wanted to wake from.

He turned me gently to face him. "So, Miss Larissa, how long do I get you for?"

I shrugged. Tears welled in my eyes, not from sadness, but from the overwhelming beauty of the moment. I reached up and cuped his face, pulling him down for another kiss, this one slow and tender. "As long as you want."

That's how I met Vladimir Kensington.

He took me to his apartment that night after I admitted that I had nowhere else to stay while in town, and he was more than happy to offer me his place. Vlad disappeared for a moment and came back with a clean t-shirt and shorts for me to wear. "It might be a little big on you, but the shorts have a drawstring."

I blushed. "That was thoughtful. Thank you." I found the bathroom and changed. When I came out I plopped down on the couch and grimaced.

"Is it that bad?" he asked.

"Well, it wasn't that good," I said awkwardly.

Vlad sat next to me and attempted to squish into the couch. "This really sucks."

A laugh burst from me. "It really does."

"I'm so sorry, I don't usually sit out on it. Honestly, I didn't realize it was so…" Vlad trailed off. "Hard." He ran his hand through his hair. "You can have the bed."

"It's okay, I don't want to put you out," I said with a smile. "I'm happy for the couch."

"Would you like a cup of tea?" he offered.

My chest warmed. "Yes, thank you."

Settling into a comfortable conversation was easy and stretched into the night.

I learned about his family back in the United Kingdom—two sisters and an older brother he doesn't see often. His parents had passed away years ago, leaving him with a mix of fond memories and unresolved silences. He shared his passion for soccer, or football, as he insisted on calling it, recounting games he had played and matches he had watched.

Every detail we exchanged seemed to draw us closer; I felt a connection to him that was surprisingly quick but profound. As the sky began to lighten, I found the courage to tell him that I needed him—not just for tonight, but in ways I was still trying to understand.

"I've told you about the places I've been, Vlad, but there's more," I started, my voice a little shaky with the dawn. "There's something about The Arcane Room and its magic—it's like nothing else.

And none of this," I gestured around, "none of my day spent wandering this city or sitting here with you, should feel real… but it does."

He listened, his face unreadable for a moment before softening. "Even if this isn't real, it feels real to me. Why let it be anything different?" he asked quietly.

I needed to have him.

I pulled off my shirt and tugged at his, and he helped me remove it. The moment our skin connected, it was as if a swarm of butterflies took off from my stomach, tingling me in every direction.

He fumbled with my bra strap, and I reached behind my back to help him. We freed my breasts, and he held me at arm's length to admire my naked torso for the first time. He bit his lip, then pulled me in for a tight embrace, his lips met mine, moving slowly to my neck, lightning crashing through my body. He followed the contour of my clavicle, down between my breasts.

Vlad gently cupped my breasts and slowly rubbed his thumbs over my erect nipples. He kissed his way toward them, but just before his mouth made contact, he paused.

"Wait," he said.

"Everything okay?" I asked, looking down at the top of his head.

"You've been so honest with me. I owe you the same courtesy." His hands slid to my shoulders, then down to my hands. He looked me dead in the eyes and said, "There's something I need to tell you."

4

"What is it?" I asked, looking deep into Vlad's eyes.

He sighed, running a hand through his dark, perfectly quaffed hair. "I haven't had to tell someone this in a long time, Larissa."

A chill ran down my spine, but I kept my cool. This was still all part of my fantasy—right? "You can tell me anything, Vlad."

His gaze darkened, as if he were searching for something in my soul. "I'm not like other men you've met. There's something you need to know before we go any further."

I tilted my head, curiosity rising. "You're starting to worry me. Just say it."

He took a deep breath. "I'm a vampire."

I stared at him, his words hanging in the air. "A vampire? Like... Dracula?"

"Yes. But it's not a myth or fiction," he said, voice heavy with centuries of experience. "I was turned long ago, centuries in fact. I feed on blood to survive." His eyes searched mine, gauging my reaction. "But I don't kill when I feed—not anymore."

"Not anymore?" I asked, trying to process. "So, you used to?"

He nodded. "When I was younger, it was... easier to lose control. Newer vampires struggle with restraint. Drinking blood can be thrilling, intoxicating. But over time, I learned to manage the hunger." He paused, voice lowering. "But killing isn't necessary for survival. It's more... satisfying, yes, but it's a choice. A dangerous one."

A shiver ran down my spine, but the excitement swelled within me. "You don't hurt anyone now?"

"Not anymore," he said firmly. "I take only from those who deserve it. Wife-beaters, rapists, the kind of men who wouldn't be missed by anyone who matters. It's a way to feed... and balance the scales, I suppose."

I blinked, digesting the weight of his words.

This was no fantasy anymore. Yet, instead of fear, I felt a rush of excitement. "So... you won't kill me?"

His eyes softened, and he gave a small, relieved smile. "No, Larissa. I'm not going to kill you. I just wanted you to know what I am before we continue."

I stepped closer to him, my heart pounding for reasons I didn't quite understand. "So, you drink blood, but it doesn't turn me or kill me? Unless... you wanted to?"

"Exactly. Turning someone is not something taken lightly. It's... a bond, an eternal one. And I have no desire to create a fledgling vampire without good reason," he explained. "Besides, feeding doesn't hurt humans like the stories say. At least not when it's done carefully."

"So, vampires really are out there?" I asked, feeling a strange mix of awe and curiosity.

He nodded. "There are more of us than you'd think, but we keep to ourselves. We have services that cater to our needs." His lips curled slightly. "For example, there's the Blood Vine—a discreet service for vampires. They deliver blood, even blood-infused meals and drinks, all in sleek black bags, embossed with a red blood drop encircled by vines.

It's safer than taking from humans, especially in cities."

I raised an eyebrow, imagining vampires getting delivery blood. "Fancy."

"It keeps us hidden and lessens the need to hunt." His tone grew more serious, his eyes flicking toward the window as if sensing something beyond it. "But we're not without enemies. There's a group... hunters."

"Hunters?" My voice barely registered.

He nodded grimly. "They've been after us for centuries. They call themselves the Crucis Praetorium, an ancient order sworn to eradicate vampires. They know when we're weakest—during the day, when sunlight doesn't burn us but makes us slow, vulnerable. They're relentless and have become more aggressive recently. They've killed many of us."

I swallowed hard, the weight of his words sinking in. "And they're after you?"

"They're after all of us," he said quietly. "They've already taken some of my closest friends. I haven't seen one in a while, but it's only a matter of time before they strike again."

The gravity of it all hit me, but strangely, I wasn't terrified. Maybe it was the surrealism of the situation or the fantasy I had long entertained. "So, what now?"

Vlad's lips curled into a seductive smile, his earlier intensity momentarily giving way to a more playful energy. "Now, let me show you what else a vampire can do."

I reached up, cupping his face with my hands. "Show me."

He leaned in, his breath cool against my warm skin. "With pleasure," he whispered before capturing my lips in a deep kiss.

Vlad's lips pressed against mine with a hunger I hadn't felt before. His kiss was intense, almost primal, sending waves of heat coursing through my body. I melted into him, wrapping my arms around his neck, pulling him closer. His hands roamed over my back, gripping me with a possessive strength that made me gasp against his mouth.

His hands traveled the length of my back, and his hand slipped inside my panties, grabbing my bare ass.

"You look so sexy in my gym shorts," he growled through our kisses.

I took the opportunity to deepen the kiss, my tongue exploring his with a ferocity that left me breathless. I could feel the coolness of his skin contrasting with the warmth of his lips, a reminder of the supernatural nature he had just confessed. Instead of fear, it ignited a thrill within me.

Vlad's hand stayed on my ass, squeezing. It sent electricity through my entire body. His other hand slid down my sides, tracing the curves of my body, leaving a trail of goosebumps in their wake. He broke the kiss, his mouth trailing down my neck, sucking and nibbling gently at the sensitive skin. Each touch sent shivers through me, making me arch against him, craving more.

I tangled my fingers in his hair, urging him on.

"Larissa," he whispered against my collarbone, his breath hot and needy. "You have no idea what you do to me."

I could barely find my voice, my mind spinning with desire. "Show me, Vlad. Show me everything."

His lips claimed mine again, more urgent, more demanding. I responded with equal fervor, losing myself in the intoxicating mix of passion and danger. Vlad's hands roamed over my body, leaving a trail of fire in their wake. He reached down and swiftly slid the remaining clothing from my body.

Before I had time to react, he lifted me effortlessly, guiding us to the nearest surface.

He laid me down gently, hovering over me, his

eyes dark and full of longing. "You are exquisite," he whispered, his voice deep and resonant. The warmth of his breath against my skin sent shivers down my spine.

I reached up, pulling him down to me, needing to feel the weight of him. With a growl of satisfaction, he kissed me again, pouring centuries of longing and loneliness as he kissed my neck. Our bodies moved together, lusting for more, lost in the ecstasy of the moment. The world ceased to exist, and all that mattered was the connection between us, the undeniable pull of destiny and desire.

Vlad moved with an intensity and determination. Before I could stress about the curves of my body on display before this god of a man, he began worshiping them. He started by kissing my stomach, his lips tracing the soft, round contours with a reverence that made my heart swell. Each kiss was a testament to his desire, affirming the sexuality of my curves.

"You are so beautiful," he murmured against my skin, his voice rough with emotion. His hands explored every inch of me, his touch both gentle and possessive, making me feel cherished and wanted. He admired the softness of my body, his fingers lingering on my hips and thighs, squeezing gently to feel the fullness there.

With a lustful growl, Vlad shifted lower, his breath hot against my wet center. The anticipation coiled tightly within me, each breath a shaky intake as I waited for him to claim me. His tongue found my delicate folds, exploring slowly at first, then with increasing urgency as he found my pleasure nub.

His mouth worked imagic, running circles around my clit, sending waves of pleasure radiating through me. Each movement brought me closer to the edge, the coiling tension in my center tightening with every pass of his tongue.

I arched against him, my hands finding his hair and pulling him closer, urging him to deepen the exquisite torment. "Vlad," I gasped, my voice a mix of plea and command.

He looked up at me through hooded eyes, his gaze intense as he continued his fervent worship. Suddenly, he shifted, positioning himself at my entrance. With one deep growl, he entered me, filling me completely, his thick length stretching me in the most delicious way.

The world narrowed to the sensation of him moving within me, each thrust bringing me closer to oblivion. "Your curves are perfect," he growled as he watched the way our bodies joined, his hands roaming over my hips, guiding the rhythm. "You fit me so perfectly, every lush curve of yours is a siren's call."

As he thrust deeper, his fingers found my clit again, circling with a relentless pace. The building pleasure was almost too much, each wave higher and more intense than the last. He kissed me fiercely, his lips devouring my cries of ecstasy, his tongue dueling with mine as he drove me over the edge.

The climax hit me like a tidal wave, crashing over me with such force that my vision blurred. My body clenched around him, the waves of my release milking him, pulling him deeper. "Vlad!" I screamed, my voice breaking with the intensity of my orgasm.

He followed soon after, his movements becoming erratic as he reached his own peak. With a final, deep growl, he spilled into me, his hot release filling me as he collapsed on top of me, his breath ragged in my ear.

We lay there, wrapped in each other's arms, the aftershocks of our passion rippling through us. Vlad's hands continued to trace slow, soothing patterns on my back, his lips pressing tender kisses to my forehead.

"You are everything," he whispered, his voice thick with emotion. "Every curve, every breath, every moan—perfect."

The connection we shared in those moments, wrapped in the warmth of each other's embrace under the canopy of night, was something profound, transcending the boundaries of fantasy and reality.

Vlad grinned an evil grin. "You liked that?"

"Yes," I said.

"Say *yes sir*," he demanded.

"Yes sir," I said. I was taken aback by the command and by how much I enjoyed being commanded.

He kissed down my center to my throbbing pussy. His tongue lapping at my swollen folds. My breathing became rapid, and I grabbed the back of his head with a handful of his hair, shoving him deeper into me.

I dragged his face to mine, and we kissed deeply. His tongue was warm and wet from being inside of me.

"You like that?" I asked him back, mocking his accent.

"Very much so," he said.

"Say, *very much so, mistress,*" I said and bit my tongue at him.

"Very much so, mistress," he said as he grabbed at still erect manhood, stroking it. "Does mistress want this cock again?"

"Very much so, sir," I said.

Vlad grabbed me by my thighs and pulled me towards him as effortlessly as moving a pillow. I slid over the silky bedsheets with ease, as he moved on top of me. Our lips met again, and my breath was forced out of me as his shaft slid into me.

He moved slowly this time. The feeling of him inside was more intimate this time. Vlad thrusted, slowly and gently. He let out soft moans as he picked up speed.

He sank into me and paused.

"I want you on top, I want to see all of you as you ride my cock, mistress."

"Yes sir," I said as we flipped over with him still inside of me. My knees straddling the sides of him.

He put one arm behind his head, stretching out his abs and pecs which glistened with a coating of sweat. I ran my hand over his rock-hard stomach and ran my fingers through the hairs of his treasure trail.

I started thrusting my hips, feeling him slide in and out of my pussy. I reached down with my other hand and rubbed at my nub. Faster and faster. I found my stride, my body convulsed from the inside.

"I'm gonna cum," I said between labored breaths.

"Fuck yes, cum for me, mistress," he said.

His words sent me over the edge, quivering and convulsing on top of him. The rush of release moved through my body. I screamed out "Fuuuu-uck," as I came with him deep inside of me. I collapsed on top of him, my legs too weak to keep me upright. He rolled me gently to my side and pulled out of me.

A few strokes of his shaft and he covered me with his hot jizz, moaning as he unloaded onto my thighs.

"That was fucking hot, Larissa. I mean, mistress," he said directly into my ear.

We laid together, his arms wrapping around me in a tight embrace. Eventually, he managed to wrap us in a blanket.

"Are you sure you don't want to clean us up first?" I asked.

"No, mistress, I don't mind laying in our mess,"

he said and pulled me closer. The wet spots now cold. We held each other close until I drifted into a deep sleep.

I had no sense of how long I was out, but when I awoke, Vlad was no longer beside me. I assumed he had gotten up to let me rest, given that he never sleeps. I sat up, rubbing the sleep from my eyes. The scent of something savory filled the air, drawing me towards the kitchen. I slipped out of bed, still groggy, and padded across the room. I noticed a pile of clothes neatly laid out for me.

I threw on a shirt and some shorts and made my way into the kitchen. There was Vlad, standing at the stove, moving with graceful precision as he prepared food. His movements were effortless, as if even something as simple as cooking required a level of finesse beyond my own comprehension. He turned slightly, his eyes locking onto mine.

"You're awake," he said with a smile. "I thought you might be hungry when you woke up."

I couldn't help but grin back as I leaned against the counter. "Starving."

Vlad winked, plating an omelet that was covered in cheese. "Here, a ham and cheese omelet before we head out."

"Head out?" I asked, taking the plate from him.

Vlad's expression softened, but there was a glimpse of something beneath the surface, excitement maybe? "I want you to meet a few of my friends."

I raised an eyebrow, taking a bite of the food. It was perfect, naturally. "Where are we going?"

"A special vampire hotel," he said. "It's... different than what you're probably imagining. But trust me, you'll like it."

The idea of stepping deeper into Vlad's world intrigued me, but it also made my pulse quicken. Meeting more vampires wasn't exactly on my to-do list. Yet, there was something about Vlad's calm confidence that put me at ease.

5

"You don't need to be worried," Vlad said, looking at my face, clearly sensing my unease.

"Sorry, I just…" I searched for the right words. When I pictured a vampire den, I imagined something dark, dreary, and almost crypt-like. But this… this was something else entirely. "This just isn't how I imagined it."

Vlad smiled, his hand warm and reassuring as he gently took mine. "It surprises most people at first." We moved past the lobby, the air thick with a subtle scent of sandalwood and aged wood. The entire place was... luxurious. Opulent, even. Not a crypt. Not a den. "Welcome to the Bloodvine Hotel."

I blinked, trying to take it all in. The sprawling, pristine marble floors, the sweeping staircases, the soft hum of music drifting through the air. "A hotel?"

"Not just any hotel," Vlad said with a sly grin. "It's more like a sanctuary. A place where vampires can gather, enjoy each other's company, and indulge in the finer things immortality has to offer."

We passed through a grand archway, and I felt a shiver crawl down my spine. "What was that?"

"Wards," Vlad explained, his tone casual. "Powerful magic woven into the very fabric of this building to keep humans at bay. You could say it's exclusive." His eyes twinkled with amusement. "You're only here because I brought you."

"So, it's not really for safety from hunters then?" I asked, recalling his earlier mention of danger.

He shook his head. "The wards protect us from prying human eyes, but the hunters are another story. They're relentless, but here…" He gestured to the space around us. "Here, we're not running from them. We don't cower. We live. We thrive."

The grandeur of the hotel seemed to expand with every step. Golden chandeliers hung from towering ceilings, casting a soft, warm glow over the space. Rich velvet drapes framed windows that weren't windows at all—just projections of sunlight. Every detail screamed luxury. "This place is incredible," I whispered.

Vlad's grip on my hand tightened, pulling me closer as he kissed the back of it. "We gather here because eternity is long, Larissa. And when you live forever, you learn to appreciate the finer things. Comfort. Beauty. Companionship. That's why we're here—not because we're afraid."

I smiled despite myself. His confidence, the richness of his world—it was intoxicating.

He gestured toward a large set of double doors, which opened silently before us. Inside was a room that rivaled the lobby in grandeur. Plush leather armchairs were arranged in intimate clusters, while a roaring fireplace crackled in the center, giving the space a sense of warmth that felt almost... human. Deep burgundy walls were lined with bookshelves, filled with ancient tomes and modern novels alike. A grand piano stood off to one side, untouched but gleaming in the firelight.

"This," Vlad said, gesturing around us, "is where we gather. It's not about safety in numbers. It's about indulgence. Vampires are social creatures, and eternity is far more enjoyable when you share it."

I let my gaze sweep over the room. I had never imagined vampires living like this—bathing in luxury, basking in the elegance of time itself. "I've spent my life believing vampires were monsters hiding in the dark."

Vlad smirked, brushing a strand of hair from my face. "You'll find there's more to our kind than the stories would have you believe."

I sank into a nearby chaise lounge, its velvet cushions wrapping around me like a lover's embrace. The plush furniture, the scent of lavender and wood, the opulent chandeliers—it was all intoxicating. "This is… beyond anything I imagined."

Vlad settled beside me, his fingers tracing patterns along my arm. "You'll come to find that vampires, in many ways, are simply connoisseurs of life. We enjoy what the human world has to offer—but we live without its limitations. Luxury, art, music, pleasure—it's all ours, forever."

Just then, the door swung open, and a small group of vampires entered, their presence commanding attention.

The first was a woman with fiery red hair cascading down her back. Her emerald eyes gleamed with mischief, her sleek black dress hugging every curve as she moved with feline grace.

Next was a man with quiet intensity in his dark eyes, his suit tailored to perfection. There was a rugged charm about him, and yet, an undeniable elegance that softened his edges. Then came a petite woman, her silver pixie cut giving her an air of youthful rebellion, and a fourth vampire, her dark curls and calm confidence making her every step feel like a dance.

But it was the last vampire who truly stole my breath. Her midnight black hair flowed like a waterfall, and her violet eyes locked onto me with a gaze so intense, it was as if she could see through my soul. Her deep crimson dress clung to her figure, radiating an almost ethereal beauty.

Vlad stood, extending his hand to her. "Larissa, this is Natasha, the matriarch of our little community."

Natasha's smile was soft yet commanding as she approached. "It's a pleasure to meet you, Larissa," she said, her voice like silk. "Vlad speaks very highly of you."

Her hand was cool as it met mine, and for a moment, I was struck speechless. Everything about her—the way she moved, the way she spoke—was mesmerizing.

"We're not like humans, Larissa," Vlad continued. "We don't cower in fear, hiding from the world. We live in it, alongside it, in ways humans can't imagine. And places like this hotel—this sanctuary—allow us to do so in style." His lips brushed against my hand once more, sending a spark through my veins. "Eternity offers pleasures that mortals can only dream of."

Natasha's presence was comforting, an unexpected balm to my frayed nerves. She seemed to sense my unease, her fingers gently tracing circles on the back of my hand as we stood together. Normally, this would be awkward and uncomfortable with someone I had just met, but with Natasha, it felt as natural as breathing.

"I know this must all be overwhelming," she said, her voice smooth. "But you are safe here, with us."

I nodded, trying to find my footing in this bizarre new reality. "It's just a lot to take in," I admitted, glancing around at the other vampires who were now engaged in quiet conversation.

Natasha's eyes softened. "I understand. It wasn't so different for me when I first joined them. Vlad was such a wonderful friend to me. Still is. I don't know what I would do without him."

Her words were somehow reassuring. "How

long have you been… here?" I asked, gently and genuinely curious about her story.

"A long time." A wistful smile played on Natasha's lips. "There's something special about you. Vlad speaks very highly of you."

My cheeks flushed slightly at the mention of Vlad. "He does?"

Natasha nodded, her gaze unwavering. "Yes, he sees something in you. And so do I."

We spent the next few moments chatting about my time with Vlad. I found myself gravitating to her like a magnet. I absorbed her presence. Natasha was infectious.

"Would you like to see the rest of our hotel?" Her smile was inviting.

"I'd love to," I said, grateful for the distraction and the opportunity to get some more alone time with her.

Natasha led me through the spacious, quaint rooms, each one more luxurious than the last. She pointed out the various amenities—a grand library filled with ancient texts, a music room with a grand piano under a gleaming chandelier, and a garden room with lush greenery and a trickling fountain.

"This place is incredible," I breathed, feeling a

sense of awe at the beauty and sophistication of it all.

"It is," Natasha agreed, her eyes beaming with pride. "It can get lonely without others of our kind. It's more than just a haven. It's our daytime home, our community. We spend a lot of time here, especially during the long days of summer."

A warmth spread through me. "That makes sense." A gently trickling waterfall greeted us in a garden room under a large fern. I closed my eyes and let the Zen wash over.

When I opened my eyes, Natasha had moved closer. She reached out and ran her hand up my arm. "You're quite beautiful, Larissa."

My cheeks flushed red. "Thank you. You are the stunning one, though."

She squeezed my hand gently and leaned in closer, pausing a few inches from my face. I wanted to meet her halfway, to taste her, but something stopped me.

"Vlad," I whispered.

"Vlad is a wonderful guy," she whispered back.

"I… I was with him. Like, together. We…" I was so drunk on her presence, I struggled for the words.

"I know," Natasha said. "He said you were fucking delicious. He thought I might love you too."

"Really?" I said, slightly confused.

"Yes," Natasha assured me. "Vampires aren't as concerned with monogamous love as you humans are. We love freely and openly."

"Oh?" I said, my eyes closed with Natasha still a small lean away.

"Absolutely," she whispered. I leaned forward and Natasha pulled me in. Our lips met for a soft, pillowy kiss. It was like kissing a perfect cloud. Her tongue traced the seam of my lips, seeking entrance, and I parted them willingly, allowing her to explore. The taste of her was intoxicating, a mix of sweetness and something darker, more mysterious. I was completely lost to the sensation.

Natasha's kiss intensified, filled with a passion that took my breath away. Her hands moved to the back of my neck, her fingers tangling in my hair as our tongues danced. I explored her mouth with my own and savored every single moment.

Natasha's lips were soft but demanding, guiding me to a gentle rhythm that made my thrum. She equally as intense as with Vlad, but a thousand times gentler somehow. Every touch, every caress, was a promise of the wild, unrestrained love she had spoken of. I found myself responding eagerly, matching her passion as our bodies pressed closer together.

My hands roamed over her back, feeling the smoothness of her dress and the firmness of her muscles beneath. She moaned softly into my mouth, the sound vibrating through me. My arousal heightened, I wanted more. I needed more, more of this incredible connection. Of this Aphrodite of a woman.

Natasha broke the kiss only to trail her lips down my neck, leaving fire in her wake. I gasped, my hands gripping her shoulders as she found the sensitive spot just below my ear. Her fangs graced my skin, not piercing instead dragging along the length of my neck, which sent hot shivers down my spine.

Danger and passion collided.

"Larissa," she murmured against my skin, her voice husky with desire. "You have no idea how much I want you right now."

6

I pulled Natasha into a kiss, desperate to feel her lips on mine once more. Our kisses grew more fervent, urgent, as if we were trying to merge our very beings. The world around us faded away, leaving only the two of us in this moment of raw, unbridled passion.

There was a bond between us. As if our souls were intertwining. A connection that went beyond the physical. I knew then that I was falling for her, deeply and irrevocably. It scared and excited me all at once.

Natasha's hands slid up my back, her fingers cool as they ventured to my hair. She pulled me even closer, our bodies pressed together so tightly that I could feel the rhythmic beat of her heart against my chest. Her lips moved against mine with a hunger that matched my own, and I lost myself in the taste of her, in the electric charge that flowed between us.

As our kisses deepened, Natasha's touch grew tender, more deliberate. Her hands trailed down my arms. She paused for a moment, her lips hovering against mine, her breath mixing with mine in the small space between us. Her eyes, glowed with a mysterious delight, locking onto mine. In that instant, it was as if she could see into the deepest parts of me, the parts I had kept hidden for so long.

"Larissa," she whispered, her voice a soft caress. "Do you feel it too? This connection between us?"

I nodded, unable to speak, my thoughts a whirl of emotions and sensations. I had never felt this way before—so intense, so consuming. It was as if Natasha had awakened something within me. It was powerful and primal, and I didn't know whether to embrace it or run from it.

But there was no running now. Not from this. Not from her.

"I feel it," I whispered back, my voice trembling with the weight of truth. "And it scares me… but I also don't want it to stop."

Natasha smiled, a mix of tenderness and something darker. Something more dangerous. She leaned in, her lips brushing against my ear as she whispered, "Then let's not stop."

Her words held a promise. I kissed her again, pouring every ounce of my longing, desire, and my fear into the kiss. She grabbed my hand and led me to a large white couch on the other side of the atrium. She set me down and climbed on top of me.

Her kisses moved down the side my neck, just under my earlobes. Her hands tickled at the bottom of my shirt, touching the soft skin of my stomach, letting a finger or two poke underneath. Her kisses moved down my neck towards my chest.

Natasha's fingers traced delicate patterns on my skin, sliding under my shirt. She lifted the hem of my shirt, her lips following the path of her hands, leaving a trail of warmth that contrasted with the coolness of her touch. When her mouth reached the center of my chest.

"You're so sensitive," Natasha said, her sultry voice, sending another wave of heat through me. Her lips curled into a teasing smile as she leaned back down, her mouth brushing lightly over my collarbone. My heart fluttered.

Her hands grazed the curve of my waist. Natasha tugged gently at my shirt, silently asking for permission, and I responded by lifting my arms. She pulled it over my head and tossed it aside.

Natasha's eyes roamed over my bare skin, and the intensity of her gaze made me feel exposed in the most exhilarating way. Her lips found their way to my stomach, her kisses growing deeper, more possessive. She was claiming me with every touch.

Natasha let out a soft hum of approval as she tugged my skirt down, pulling my panties along with it. She continued her exploration, her lips venturing lower, tracing the lines of my stomach and the dip to my center.

Slipping between my legs, Natasha slung my right leg over her shoulder, the weight settling against her with a thud. She moved her concentration to my inner thigh, kissing and delivering teasing bites all the way up my leg. The sensation was too much to bear, and I let out a soft scream. I clasped my hands over my mouth to stifle it.

"You can be as loud as you want in here, Larissa," she motioned towards the door with her eyes. "No one can hear us."

Natasha found my slit, her tongue made gentle swirling motions, lapping at my folds. She found my swollen clit. She tongued at it as she slid two fingers inside of me, making me gasp. She pulled out of me bringing her fingers to her lips, covering them in her saliva before thrusting them back into me, wiggling as she went. My back arched off the couch and she thrusted harder into my pussy, she lapped at my clit sending me closer to the edge.

Her tongue explored my folds, her fangs scraping gently across my flesh.

I was close.

"Slow down, I'm about to cum," I managed to eke out.

"No," she growled back. Natasha's fingers moved inside of me. "You will come for me."

I began involuntarily thrusting with the rhythm of her fingers, her face, harder, and harder.

My breath gone.

My toes curled.

I let out a primal scream, my legs, trembling, were still resting on Natasha's shoulders. She didn't quit though; she kept her mouth and fingers focused on my clit as I writhed and shook with the pulsating orgasm.

My body went limp. She moved to meet my mouth for a kiss, the taste of me still fresh on her lips.

"That's a good girl," she growled.

"I don't think I have ever cum that hard before," I managed between breaths.

"That's because you hadn't met me yet," Natasha said.

I pulled my skirt back up, composing myself. Natasha located my shirt, strewn across the atrium and brought it to me. She raked her fingers through my sex head hair.

"They're going to know something happened," I laughed.

"Let them," Natasha teased, her voice dripped satisfaction. She handed me my shirt, and I quickly slipped it on, still feeling the lingering warmth of her inside of me.

As we made our way back to the main room, I could feel the adrenaline slowly ebbing, replaced by nervousness. When we entered the room, Vlad was lounging casually on one of the luxurious sofas, a glass of deep red wine in his hand. At least I like to think it was wine. He glanced up as we approached.

"Ah," he said, his lips curling into a knowing smile. "I see you two have been getting acquainted." There was no jealousy in his tone, only a hint of amusement and perhaps even pride.

Natasha leaned against the back of a chair; her gaze locked with Vlad's. "We were just bonding."

Vlad chuckled, setting his glass down on the table. "I'm glad to hear it. Larissa, you're in good hands here," he said. "Natasha has a way of making people feel welcome."

I couldn't help but smile, the tension easing as I realized there was no judgment, only acceptance. The room felt warmer, more inviting, as if the connection I'd just experienced with Natasha had somehow deepened my bond with this strange, alluring world I'd stumbled into.

A loud thud echoed through the lobby as the door swung open. A man stumbled in, collapsing at our feet. His body was beaten and bloodied, his clothes torn and stained with dirt and blood.

7

"What happened?" Vlad demanded, his voice tight, kneeling beside the barely conscious man.

"Crucis," the man gasped between ragged breaths.

"Were you followed?" Vlad's voice cut through the room like a blade as Natasha and Marcus darted to the door, their movements fast and precise, making sure no one else had entered.

The man shook his head weakly. "No..." he managed, before collapsing unconscious.

"Rebecca, get blood," Vlad ordered, his tone sharp as Rebecca disappeared down the hall. "Help me get him on the couch."

Without a word, Irina scooped the man up effortlessly, her vampire strength on full display as she laid him gently on the plush leather sofa. The ease with which she moved reminded me that these were not fragile beings, despite the gravity of the situation. I stood frozen, feeling utterly useless as the vampires worked with efficient speed.

Rebecca returned with a sleek black bag, the crimson emblem of the Blood Vine service on its side—a blood drop encircled by vines. She pulled out a bottle of blood and held it to the man's lips, coaxing him to drink.

Natasha appeared beside me, her voice soft but controlled. "Are you alright?"

I nodded, trying to find my voice. "Are we okay? What... what's happening?"

"The hunters," Natasha replied, locking eyes with Vlad, her gaze unflinching. "They're getting closer. It might be wise to split into smaller groups for now. Safety in numbers doesn't always apply to us. Vlad, you and Larissa can stay at my place tonight."

Rebecca chimed in, already standing by Marcus's side. "Zoya and Marcus can stay with me."

Zoya crossed her arms, shooting Rebecca a look. "I'm going with Irina. It's smarter if we stay in pairs, but I don't need babysitting."

Vlad nodded. "That makes sense. What about Michael?" he asked, glancing at the unconscious man on the couch.

A moment of hesitation hung in the air before Rebecca spoke, her voice quiet. "We do what we can for him, but we can't bring him with us. He's a liability in this condition."

"That's cold," Zoya snapped, her eyes narrowing. "He's one of us."

"And we're all targets now," Rebecca shot back, her fiery hair catching the low light. "Do you want to explain to the Crucis why we're dragging around someone who can't defend himself?"

Zoya's jaw tightened, but she didn't argue. The reality of the situation was clear.

"Alright," Vlad said, his voice steady but filled with authority. "We have twenty minutes before sunset. Let's wrap this up and leave in intervals. We can't take any risks."

The group moved with practiced efficiency, a routine they had clearly performed before. There was no hesitation, no panic, just cold, calculated action. I watched as Irina and Zoya exchanged a glance before slipping out into the night, their movements so fluid and graceful that they seemed more like shadows than people. Rebecca and Marcus followed, disappearing just as swiftly.

Michael remained on the couch, his breathing shallow but stable. Vlad knelt beside him for a moment, murmuring something I couldn't hear before standing. He gave Natasha a nod, signaling it was time for us to leave.

"Let's move," Vlad said, his tone low but commanding.

Natasha took my hand, and together we followed Vlad out of the Bloodvine Hotel. The night air was cool and crisp, a stark contrast to the warmth of the luxurious interior we had just left behind. We moved swiftly through the city streets, darting in and out of alleyways, our pace fast but not panicked. Despite the tension in the air, there was a thrill coursing through me. I was moving through the night with two powerful vampires by my side, and the adrenaline of it all was intoxicating.

Vlad led the way, his movements fluid and confident, while Natasha stayed close to me, her hand never leaving mine. The city felt distant, almost dreamlike, as we moved through it like predators in the night. Every sound, every flicker of light, seemed irrelevant compared to the energy that pulsed between us.

After what felt like only moments, we arrived at Natasha's home. It was a tall, elegant townhouse tucked away in a quiet corner of the city, its ivy-covered stone walls and large, softly glowing windows a picture of old-world charm and modern luxury.

Natasha opened the door, ushering me inside. The interior was as breathtaking as the exterior—high ceilings, rich dark wood, and plush fabrics surrounded us in warmth. A crystal chandelier glittered above, casting soft light across the grand staircase that spiraled up to the upper floors.

"This is... incredible," I breathed, taking it all in.

Natasha smiled, her hand still holding mine as she led me further inside. "Welcome to my sanctuary. Please, make yourself at home."

Vlad closed the door behind us, his presence filling the space with a quiet sense of authority. "You'll be safe here," he reassured, his eyes scanning the room before landing on me.

As we moved deeper into Natasha's home, the

awe I felt only grew. Every detail was perfect—the opulence of the décor, the subtle scent of lavender and leather, the warmth of the space. It was a place of power and beauty, not unlike Natasha herself.

"We do have a minor issue," Natasha said, breaking the silence.

Vlad raised an eyebrow. "Oh?"

"We don't have any food for the human," Natasha teased, her smile playful.

I waved it off, though my stomach growled at the thought. "I'll be fine. You don't need to worry about me."

"Nonsense," Vlad said, already turning toward the door. "I'll go grab something."

I stepped forward, grabbing his arm. "No. You're not going back out there tonight. I can survive until morning. Besides, I can go out during the day. Obviously, the hunters aren't after me."

Natasha raised an eyebrow, smiling in agreement. "She has a point."

Vlad sighed, his expression conflicted. "I don't like it, but there's a market nearby. Are you sure you'll be okay?"

I smirked, glancing between him and Natasha, their strong, sleek bodies standing close. "I think I'll be just fine."

Vlad's lips twitched into a grin, and he exchanged a glance with Natasha. "Well then, we've got something else that might satisfy you in the meantime."

8

Natasha led the way, her grip on my hand firm yet gentle. As we moved through the elegant corridors of her home, the atmosphere shifted. The light dimmed, the air grew cooler, and the opulent surroundings seemed to take on a darker, more intimate energy, as if we were descending into a deeper layer of Natasha's world—one steeped in shadow and desire.

We reached a heavy wooden door at the end of the hall, intricately carved with swirling patterns and symbols that felt ancient, almost arcane. Natasha pushed it open effortlessly, revealing a space that left me breathless.

The room was vast, but it felt intimate, cloaked

in deep shadows that seemed to pulse with energy. The walls were a rich, velvety black, accented with deep red drapes cascading from ceiling to floor. Dim sconces and a grand chandelier cast a soft, golden glow, creating an ambiance that was both seductive and mysterious.

In the center of the room stood a massive bed, draped in dark, silken sheets that shimmered under the low light. The bed was framed by an ornate wrought-iron canopy, twisting like vines—giving the piece a Gothic feel. Despite the darkness of the room, the bed exuded warmth and luxury, inviting and undeniably feminine. Plush pillows, soft furs, and velvet throws were layered on it, while intricate lace detailing hinted at Natasha's delicate but dominant tastes.

The room held Natasha's essence—a blend of power and elegance. A large antique mirror with a gilded frame reflected the low light, while an intricately carved vanity and hauntingly beautiful artwork adorned the walls. There was a sophistication here, something timeless that spoke to centuries of taste and refinement, yet it also hinted at passion and control—qualities that felt inherently vampiric.

Vlad entered quietly, closing the door behind him, and the three of us stood in the center of the room. The energy between us crackled with anticipation. Natasha's eyes met mine, her gaze filled with a potent mix of desire and something deeper—a shared understanding that transcended words.

"This is my sanctuary," Natasha said, her voice a purr that sent a ripple of excitement through me. "A place where I can be myself… where we can be ourselves."

She moved closer, her fingers brushing against my arm as she circled me slowly, her touch electric. Vlad stepped forward as well, his presence grounding yet no less intense. The weight of the moment pressed down on me in the most delicious way.

Natasha's hand slid up my back, resting at the nape of my neck as she leaned in, her lips brushing against my cheek. "Are you ready to surrender to us again?" she whispered.

I turned to face her, and without hesitation, our lips met. The kiss was deep, consuming. Vlad's hand found the small of my back, pulling me closer as we moved toward the bed, leaving the world behind.

In this dark, luxurious space, surrounded by velvet and shadows, I felt myself giving in completely. This was no mere room—it was a realm of transformation, where passions ruled and the boundaries between us blurred.

The vampires threw me onto the bed, and I sunk into the soft, inviting mattress. Vlad pulled off his shirt, revealing his sculpted, pale torso. Every muscle was defined, his body the picture of immortal perfection. The dim light played off the contours of his chest, highlighting his strength.

Natasha unbuttoned her shirt, revealing a black lace bra that accentuated her ample curves. Her body was strong yet supple, her movements fluid as she turned to face Vlad, who helped her remove the rest of her clothes. His fingers trailed between her breasts and down to her navel before swiftly removing her pants, leaving her in nothing but her underwear.

Vlad grabbed Natasha by the back of her head, pulling her into a kiss. His other hand slid down her back and into her underwear, gripping her firmly as their lips moved with raw, unbridled passion. The sight of these powerful beings losing themselves to desire ignited something deep inside me. I slid my hand down, reaching beneath my skirt to touch myself as I watched them.

Vlad broke the kiss, his eyes locking onto mine.

"Not yet," he said with a teasing smirk. "That pleasure is for us to give."

I smiled back coyly, pulling my hand away, content to watch the display of power and lust in front of me.

Vlad removed the last of his clothing, revealing his hardened cock. Natasha, never breaking eye contact with me, fell to her knees before him. She reached out, guiding him into her mouth, all while her gaze remained fixed on mine.

"You like that, Larissa?" she asked, her voice sultry.

"Fuck yes," I breathed, my body already on fire.

"Should I continue?" Natasha's voice dripped with seduction.

I glanced at Vlad, his face twisted with pleasure, then back to her. "Absolutely."

Natasha continued, her movements slow and deliberate, taking him deeper into her throat. The sight of her lips wrapped around him sent a wave of heat through me. Vlad's moans filled the room as Natasha worked him with her mouth, her hands gripping his thighs as she refused to release him.

"Do you want a taste?" she asked, guiding Vlad's cock toward me.

I nodded, my body already moving forward as

they came closer. Natasha gathered my hair with one hand and gently pushed Vlad's cock into my mouth with the other. The taste of him, mingled with Natasha, was intoxicating.

"Take him deeper," Natasha whispered, her voice soft but commanding.

I did as she asked, moving my head as Vlad's moans grew louder. His pleasure was evident, and the power I felt in that moment was electrifying. I looked up at him, his eyes half-closed, his body trembling with need.

Out of the corner of my eye, I noticed Natasha fastening a pink strap-on around her waist. "I've got a little toy," she said with a mischievous smile, running her hands along the bright pink shaft.

"For me?" I asked, curiosity mixing with desire.

"Not unless you ask very nicely," Natasha teased. "This is for Vlad."

"For me?" Vlad's eyes widened in surprise, though the grin on his face betrayed his excitement.

Natasha slapped her hand against the pink shaft. "Yes, but only if you call me Daddy."

"Yes, Daddy," Vlad said, his voice thick with desire.

Natasha slicked the pink dildo with lube and

positioned herself behind Vlad. "Come sit on my face, Larissa," Vlad commanded.

I moved quickly, positioning myself over his mouth, and as I did, Natasha lifted his muscular thighs over her shoulders, exposing him completely. The intimacy of the moment, the raw vulnerability of Vlad, heightened everything. Natasha worked her fingers into him, preparing him, and Vlad moaned into me, sending shivers of pleasure through my body.

"Are you ready for Daddy's cock?" Natasha asked, her tone authoritative.

"Yes, Daddy," Vlad replied, his voice muffled against me.

Natasha slid the pink dildo into him, thrusting gently at first, and I watched as his body tensed and then relaxed, overwhelmed by the pleasure. His moans vibrated through my core, and I could feel his cock pulsing with arousal.

I slid down his body, positioning myself over his cock and taking him inside me. The sensation of him filling me as Natasha penetrated him was beyond anything I had experienced. The rhythm of our bodies moving together, the sounds of pleasure filling the room, created a symphony of lust and power.

The tension between us built, our thrusts becoming more frantic, more desperate. I could feel Vlad reaching his climax, his body trembling beneath mine, and as he came inside me, I was pushed over the edge, my own orgasm crashing through me like a wave.

Natasha pulled me into a deep kiss, her lips igniting another round of convulsions through my body. As we collapsed onto the bed, our breaths coming in ragged gasps, we lay together, the heat of the moment still lingering in the air.

Vlad smiled up at us, his body spent. "Round two?" he asked, a wicked grin on his lips.

9

Days turned into weeks, but the passing time did not weaken our resolve. We stayed hidden, biding our time, learning to move cautiously, but never out of fear. Life carried on, and though we stayed low for a while, we knew that we couldn't hide forever. The hunters were relentless, but we were not cowards. We adapted, waiting for the right moment to strike back. There was no running from this—it was our reality.

By day, I roamed the streets, gathering supplies and overhearing rumors, always on alert for any signs of the Crucis Praetorium. I felt the weight of the vampire world pressing on me with each step, walking among humans who were unaware of the darkness just below the surface. Despite the calm exterior, I knew something was stirring, a tension building that hinted at something much bigger. Every time I left Natasha's sanctuary, there was a flicker of uncertainty. But I refused to let it consume me. We couldn't cower forever.

The nights were filled with the strange comfort of Natasha's sanctuary. We would stay close, Vlad's protectiveness growing fiercer while Natasha remained cool and calculating. Despite the uncertainty, there was an odd sense of peace in the way we carried on. We kept our routines, yet always with one ear to the ground, waiting for the next sign of danger.

Then, one evening, as the sun dipped below the horizon, something changed.

A knock at the door—a slow, deliberate sound that made the hair on the back of my neck stand up. I glanced at Vlad and Natasha, both immediately on edge. When Vlad opened the door, a bloodstained note was stapled to it. A chill ran through the room. Who knew we were here?

I unfolded the paper, my hands trembling slightly. "Rebecca and Marcus… they're gone," I whispered, feeling the weight of the words sink into my bones.

Natasha's eyes darkened, her calm exterior cracking ever so slightly as fury flickered beneath the surface. Vlad's grip on my hand tightened, grounding me as the reality of the loss settled in. The Crucis were closer than we thought, and they were moving faster than we had anticipated.

"Is it true?" I asked, the question directed at Vlad, though my voice wavered with uncertainty. "Do we know they're really dead?"

Vlad's jaw clenched. "It's a rumor for now, but the signs are all there. No one's seen them for weeks, and they've gone silent. It's only a matter of time before we know for sure."

Natasha's gaze turned to Vlad, her eyes sharp. "If they've been taken down, it's only because the Crucis are moving in faster than we realized. We have to be smarter."

My mind raced, heart pounding with the implications of what was happening. "So what do we do now? Do we just wait for them to come for us?"

Vlad shook his head, his voice firm. "No. We don't hide, and we don't run. But we need to be cautious. We lay low for a few more days, gather more information. They can't pick us off one by one if we stay ahead of them."

Natasha moved closer, her hand brushing

against mine. "This isn't the first time we've faced hunters, Larissa. They've always been there, lurking. But there's something different this time. There's a bigger force behind it. We need to understand it before we act."

"What do you mean?" I asked, confused by her words.

"Word is, the hunters have been organizing more than usual. They're building an army, or so the rumors go. Someone powerful is pulling the strings, stirring things up in a way we haven't seen in centuries," Natasha explained, her voice laced with suspicion.

Before I could ask more, Vlad's eyes flicked to the bloodstained note still in my hand. "Who sent the message?" I asked, my voice barely above a whisper.

Natasha's gaze hardened. "It came from Dominic."

"Dominic?" I repeated, my heart racing. The name was unfamiliar, yet it carried weight. "Who is he?"

Vlad exchanged a glance with Natasha before speaking. "Dominic was once a hunter. He infiltrated their ranks years ago, but fell in love with one of our kind. He turned against the Crucis, became a spy for us, feeding us information on their movements. We thought he was lost when they caught him."

Natasha stepped forward, her voice calm but edged with steel. "He's been in hiding ever since, but it looks like he's resurfaced. This note is a warning—he's telling us that the Crucis are closing in. If he's risking his life to get this to us, it means the danger is real."

"So what do we do?" I asked, clutching the note tightly.

"We wait," Vlad said, his tone steady but firm. "For now, we can't risk moving. Dominic knows how to find us, and if there's more we need to know, he'll contact us again. But we can't rush out there blindly. The Crucis are waiting for us to make a mistake."

The weight of Vlad's words settled over me like a heavy blanket. We were safe here—for now. But the hunters were growing bolder, and this gilded sanctuary wouldn't hold forever.

Natasha squeezed my hand, her eyes softening slightly. "We'll get through this, Larissa. We've survived worse. And when the time comes, we'll be ready. We won't just survive—we'll make them pay."

Vlad nodded, his expression resolute. "We'll fight back when the time is right. But until then, we stay vigilant. Together."

As I sat there, surrounded by two of the most powerful beings I'd ever known, I felt the weight of the battle ahead settle in. There was no room for fear anymore—only strength, and the unwavering determination to protect the ones I loved.

10

When I came to, I was bathed in bright white light. My eyes stung as I opened them, blinking several times as disorientation gripped me. The remnants of the nightmare clung to me like a heavy fog, reluctant to release me from its hold. Slowly, the sterile room came into focus—the smooth white walls, the soft chaise I had been lying on.

It took a moment to realize where I was. The Arcane Room.

My heart pounded as the memories rushed back —Vlad and Natasha, the hunters, the passion, the fear. Was it all real? Were they gone? Was I alone?

I shot up from the chaise, my breath coming in ragged gasps, confusion swirling around me. My hand instinctively clutched at my chest, but all I felt was emptiness. I could still feel the lingering brush of Natasha's lips on mine, still hear Vlad's deep voice assuring me everything would be okay.

"Was it... was it all fake?" My voice barely rose above a whisper, but the question weighed heavily in the empty space.

From the shadows, a familiar figure emerged—Ms. Vesper. Her tattooed arms were crossed, her expression a maddening mix of pity and amusement. "Welcome back, dear," she said, her voice sickly sweet.

I stared at her, my mind racing, desperate to understand. "No... no, this can't be right. They were real. Why would you do this to me? Why would you put me through that?"

Ms. Vesper smiled, the dangerous glint in her eyes never faltering as she approached. "It was all your fantasy, Larissa," she said with an unsettling gentleness. "That's what the Arcane Room does. It makes your deepest desires come to life."

Her words felt like a slap to the face. "I've been gone for months," I protested, my hands trembling.

Ms. Vesper shook her head, her tone calm and composed. "No, dear. You were gone for twenty minutes in the real world." She gestured to the clock on the wall, her smile widening. "Time is a funny thing here."

I scrambled for my phone, desperate to prove her wrong. But she was right—only minutes had passed. How could that be? How could something so real, so vivid, have been nothing but an illusion? I staggered back, my heart sinking. "No," I muttered, shaking my head. "They were real. I loved them... I..."

"They felt real," Ms. Vesper corrected, her voice softening. "But that's the magic of the Arcane Room. It gives you what you crave most. The things you thought you'd never experience."

I collapsed back onto the chaise, the weight of the truth pressing down on me. How could something that felt so perfect, so deep, be nothing but an illusion? "Why?" I whispered, tears welling in my eyes. "Why would you put me through that?"

Ms. Vesper tilted her head, a faint smile still lingering. "The Three of Swords," she said, her voice calm but filled with meaning. "It's a card of deep emotional experiences. Heartbreak, sorrow... but also understanding. Sometimes we need to face the shadows of pain to fully appreciate the beauty of light. It seems your heart craved something real, even if it came with grief."

Tears spilled down my cheeks as I let her words sink in. "It was... beautiful," I whispered, a sense of loss washing over me.

Ms. Vesper extended her hand. "Come, my dear."

I took her hand, letting her lead me out of the sterile, white room and back into the familiar warmth of the store. I glanced around, disoriented by the contrast of the mundane with the intensity of the fantasy I had just left. As we approached the front, I spotted Andrew sitting on a bench at the far end of the store. I took a deep breath, wiping my face dry before walking over to him.

We exchanged a glance, both of us looking glossy-eyed, as if we'd both woken up from a dream we couldn't yet explain.

"Ready to get out of here?" I asked, my voice a little shaky.

"Yeah," Andrew replied quietly.

We said our goodbyes to Ms. Vesper, and as I slipped her some cash, she gave me a knowing smile. "Remember, Larissa, the Arcane Room reveals what's already inside you."

I stepped out into the cool air, the world outside feeling strangely unreal. I could still feel the weight of Vlad's love, Natasha's touch, and the dangers we faced together, lingering like ghosts in my mind. But it wasn't real. That part of me was back here, in this life. Jason—my boyfriend—flashed through my thoughts, and a pang of guilt followed. He could never know what happened in the Arcane Room, how deeply it had affected me. How could it not? But that was a problem for another day.

Andrew and I climbed into his car, the silence thick between us as we drove away from the shop. The tension sat heavy, neither of us ready to confront the emotions we'd just been through.

"Do you want to talk about it?" I asked after a while, my voice low.

"No," Andrew replied quickly, but then, after a pause, he added, "Do you?"

I shook my head, leaning back in the seat. "Definitely not."

We lapsed into silence again, the road stretching out before us, the world returning to its familiar rhythm. But something had shifted. The memories of Vlad and Natasha, of the life I had lived in those fleeting minutes, were still with me. And I had no idea what that would mean for my real life—or for me.

· · ·

SIGN up for Jax Wilder's newsletter and receive a collection of unpublished Coral Cove short stories. Meet familiar characters and dive deeper into the love and romance that Coral Cove is known for. Don't miss out on this exclusive content!

https://mailchi.mp/158597581671/jax-wilder

Jax Wilder

Larissa's story will continue in *Larissa's Revenge*. *While you're waiting, check out The Perfect Lover Spell.*

Accidental Magic Creates A Perfect Lover

JESSA:

The love spell I cast was supposed to be a joke.

But now a Scotsman from 2014 is in my living room.

We must reverse the magic before he's stuck here forever.

But I'm falling for the perfect lover I never expected.

BRYCE:

One moment, I'm in Scotland; the next, I'm in Jessa's world.

This love spell has bound us together.

But can we break it before I lose my heart to the enchanting woman who summoned me?

A LOVE SPELL with Unexpected Results

Jessa's love life has been a series of disasters, from awkward dates to toxic relationships. Tired of swiping left and right, she's ready to give up on finding her perfect match. But when her best friend pushes her to try something different—a love spell from the mysterious Spellbound Stories bookstore —Jessa decides to take a chance on magic. Little does she know that casting *The Perfect Lover Spell* will bring more than she bargained for.

Enter Bryce MacGregor, a handsome and rugged Scotsman who literally appears out of nowhere... from ten years in the past. Struggling to make sense of his sudden time travel, Bryce must navigate modern-day Coral Cove while Jessa tries to reverse the spell. But as they spend more time together, the line between magic and reality blurs, and sparks begin to fly.

Can Jessa and Bryce find a way to break the spell without breaking their hearts? Or has fate—and a little magic—brought them together for a reason?

The Perfect Lover Spell is a steamy, time-travel romance that blends humor, magic, and a sizzling connection that defies time itself. Perfect for fans of magical realism and heartwarming love stories.

Jax Wilder

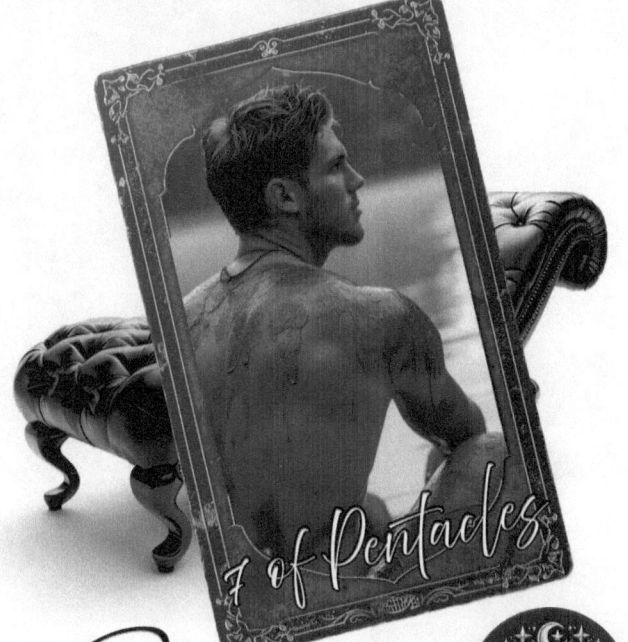

Seven of
Pentacles

Tarot Fantasies Series

SEVEN OF PENTACLES

Tarot Fantasies Series

*"**Just because I talk slow, doesn't mean I'm stupid.**" ~Jake from Sweet Home Alabama.*

Jax Wilder

7 OF PENTACLES

"With patience and persistence, you will reap the rewards of your hard work and dedication," 7 of Pentacles.

KEY WORDS AND PHRASES:

Assessment and Evaluation of progress

Patience and waiting for results

Re-evaluating goals and priorities

Long-term planning and investment

Reflecting on past efforts

Delayed gratification

Harvesting the fruits of labor

Considering alternative strategies

Taking a break to reassess

Feeling a sense of accomplishment, but still having

work to do.

Imagine you've been working really hard on something—a project, a goal, or maybe even yourself. The Seven of Pentacles is like that moment when you pause and take a breather to see how things are going. It's about asking yourself questions like, "Am I on the right track? Are my efforts paying off? Do I need to adjust my approach?"

The Seven of Pentacles isn't just about waiting around. It's about being proactive and making smart choices about where to invest your time and energy. So, when you see The Seven of Pentacles card in a reading, it's like a reminder to take stock of your progress, be patient with yourself, and keep working towards your goals. It's all about trusting the process and knowing that your efforts will pay off in the end.

—Lorelai Hamilton, author of *Teenage Tarot* and *Tarot Tales & Magic Spells*

1

It started with a tremor in my manicured hand—a slight, almost imperceptible shake as I signed off on yet another deal that would pad my already respectable bank account. But by the time I reached my corner office overlooking the New York Stock Exchange, with its grand columns and bustling atmosphere, the tremor had spread—like a crack in a vase that you can't quite believe is real until it shatters in your hands.

I'd built my life around being the best-dressed, best-connected, best-everything in the room. But it turns out, even a wardrobe full of bespoke suits and a Rolodex of power players can't save you from the inevitable—an emotional implosion in the middle of Wall Street. They called it a "nervous breakdown," but I prefer to think of it as my body staging a very dramatic coup.

The solution? Coral Cove. A place that sounds like a retirement community for people who think a wild night involves decaf coffee after 8 PM. My therapist, my boss, and everyone else who thinks they know what's best for me decided that this is where I needed to be. Apparently, when you're on the verge of becoming a cautionary tale, even the people who thrive on your success start to worry.

So here I am, banished to a seaside haven where the biggest thrill is probably a two-for-one sale on seashell necklaces. I've traded skyscrapers for sandy beaches, power lunches for—what? A quaint little café where the biggest decision is whether to order the iced tea or the lemonade?

I'll give it a week before I either lose my mind or simply pass away.

"What am I supposed to do here, Johnny?" I asked, nearly yelling into my cell phone.

"Relax. Get a massage. Go see the sights. Meet some people," he suggested.

"Meet what people? Is anyone here under ninety?" I hadn't seen a single young person in this town since I got here, three whole hours ago.

"Have you even left the hotel yet?" he asked.

I paused and sighed. "No."

Johnny gave me a few more words of encouragement before letting me get on with my evening. I was lucky to have a therapist I could call anytime—considering what I paid, it was the least he could do. I went to grab my laptop but then remembered I wasn't allowed to be on the internet while I was in Coral Cove. I was only allowed to use my phone for calls. Johnny's rules.

I huffed and tossed the laptop into a pile of clothes across the room before flopping onto the bed.

After a few minutes of staring at the ceiling, I couldn't take it anymore. The idea of spending the evening cooped up in this quaint little hotel room, with its floral wallpaper and the musty scent of decades-old furniture polish, was unbearable. With another heavy sigh, I grabbed my jacket and stepped outside, the cool evening air hitting me like a refreshing slap to the face.

The streets of Coral Cove were almost unsettling in their quietness. No honking taxis, no blaring sirens. Just the gentle hum of conversation from a nearby café and the occasional creak of an old sign swaying in the breeze. I wandered aimlessly, hands shoved in my pockets, trying to make sense of how I ended up in this sleepy seaside town.

As I walked, my eyes caught on a little shop on the corner with a windchime over the entrance. "The Arcane Room," the sign read, with ornate letters painted in a deep shade of purple. The windows were filled with strange objects—crystals, tarot cards, books with titles like *Unlocking the Mysteries of the Universe*. The kind of place that would probably appeal to those who believed in auras and chakras—things I typically scoffed at.

I shook my head, chuckling under my breath. "What is this place, a tourist trap for wannabe witches?"

Still, something about the shop tugged at my curiosity. Maybe it was the bizarre combination of the town's charm and my own boredom, but before I knew it, I was pushing open the door, a small bell jingling above my head.

The interior was exactly what I expected. Dimly lit, the smell of incense hanging heavy in the air, and shelves lining the walls with everything from tarot decks to jars of herbs. A large display case wrapped around the center of the room, covered with bowls filled with stones that supposedly held some sort of mystical power. A few candles flickered on a table near the back, casting shadows that danced across the wooden floor.

"Welcome to the Arcane Room," came a voice from behind the counter.

I turned to see a woman emerging from a curtain that separated the front of the shop from whatever lay beyond. She was seemingly ageless—forties, maybe—with dark hair pulled back into a messy bun. Bright red lipstick contrasted sharply with her pale skin. Her arms were covered in tattoos—intricate designs of moons, stars, and other symbols I didn't recognize, snaking up from her wrists to disappear underneath the sleeves of her loose, flowing blouse.

"Uh, thank you," I said, a nervous smirk tugging at the corners of my mouth.

"That is quite the suit," she said, circling me, taking me in. She chuckled softly, her eyes crinkling at the edges. "You must be a city boy who's found himself lost in our little slice of paradise."

I blinked, taken aback by her bluntness. "How'd you know?"

"Lucky guess," she said with a wink. "Or maybe it's written all over you. Either way, welcome. I am Ms. Vesper."

"Brad," I nodded at her, almost a bow. "So, what is this place? A shop for… mystical supplies?"

Ms. Vesper leaned on the counter, resting her chin in her hand. "These 'mystical supplies,'" she said, her tone teasing but not unkind, "are a collection of tools and treasures for those seeking a little more out of life. Everything here is meant to help people connect with the world around them in ways they might not have considered before."

"Right," I said, trying not to roll my eyes. "And you really believe in all this?"

Her smile softened. "Belief is a funny thing. It's not always about whether something is real or not. Sometimes, it's about the meaning we give to it. But you didn't come in here to listen to me wax philosophically, did you?"

"Honestly, I don't even know why I came in," I admitted, glancing around the shop again.

"Maybe you're looking for something you didn't know you needed," she suggested, her eyes twinkling with mischief. "Maybe you're looking for an exciting kind of experience."

I shrugged. "Maybe."

"Well," she said, pushing off the counter and moving to a table near the curtain she came from.

"How about you pull one of these tarot cards for me? Just for fun."

I hesitated, but the boredom I felt earlier was already fading, replaced by a strange sense of anticipation. "Alright," I said, surprising even myself. "Why not?"

Ms. Vesper smiled, her hands deftly shuffling the deck. "That's the spirit," she said. "Let's see what the cards have in store for you, city boy. Go ahead and draw one."

I reached out, a weird tingling sensation in my fingertips as I grabbed the first card I touched and pulled it out. I raised the card to show a man standing with a stick staring at a bunch of circles with stars in the middle.

"Ah, the Seven of Pentacles," Ms. Vesper said. "This symbolizes patience, hard work, and the fruits of your labor. It's a reminder that sometimes you need to take a step back and assess what you've sown, to see if it's truly worth the effort you've invested."

My mouth twisted slightly, one corner tugging upward in a grimace of disbelief. That definitely rang true for me, but I mean, so could any of the cards. Probably. "So, now what? Do I pull another one? What do I do with that information?"

"You get some tea," she said.

"Tea?" I raised an eyebrow at her.

"Follow me," she said, reaching out for my hand. Today was a day of new experiences, and I followed her into a white room, void of any décor aside from a large leather chaise lounge in the middle of the room.

"Sit," Ms. Vesper instructed. I did what I was told and was surprised by the softness. "The Arcane Room offers a certain experience. A magical… getaway, if you will. Have some tea, and you will be transported to your wildest fantasy. Fear not, no matter how long your experience lasts, only twenty minutes will have passed here."

She handed me the tea, and I looked up at her. This was probably how people ended up murdered. I looked back at my cup of tea, a pale yellow color that smelled like a flower bouquet. Oh well, you only live once, as the kids were saying. "Bottoms up," I said, and chugged my tea in one gulp.

2

The tea was warm, but not so hot that it burned on its way down my esophagus. The relaxation was instant. I looked over to where Ms. Vesper had been standing to hand her my cup, but she was gone. I looked down at my hand, and my cup was gone. In fact, everything was gone.

A field stretched out before me, a tangled, sodden landscape where the earth seemed to merge with the water in a murky embrace. The ground was uneven, spongy underfoot, with patches of shallow water that reflected the dull, overcast sky above. Tall reeds and cattails swayed gently in the humid breeze, their tips rustling softly like whispers from the bayou. Moss-draped cypress trees stood sentinel at the edges, their gnarled roots twisting above the surface, creating eerie, shadowed alcoves where the swamp life thrived.

The air smelled like damp earth and decaying vegetation, a heady mix that clung to the back of my throat. Every now and then, a splash echoed in the distance as something unseen disturbed the stillness of the water. The field buzzed with the incessant drone of insects, punctuated by the occasional croak of a bullfrog or the distant call of a bird. It was a place teeming with life yet steeped in an almost unsettling stillness, where time seemed to slow, and the line between water and land blurred into one endless, swampy expanse.

I looked down at my feet and saw my black shiny shoes sinking into a shadowy puddle, the wetness finally sneaking inside, drenching my socks. "Damn it, not my Pradas," I whined, lifting my soggy foot from the water only to realize there wasn't a dry place nearby to put it down.

A loud, strange sound buzzed in the distance, growing louder. I looked around to see the source, a strange boat-like object coming toward me. The boat glided over the swampy field with a strange grace, its flat deck skimming across the water's surface. The loud buzz of the fan engine filled the air, a jarring contrast to the otherwise eerie stillness of the swamp. As it drew closer, I could make out the figure aboard—a man, tall and broad-shoul-dered, his shirtless torso gleaming with a thin sheen of sweat. His overalls hung low on his hips, worn and dirty, but clinging to him in a way that suggested comfort rather than neglect.

My breath caught in my throat as the boat pulled up alongside me, the man cutting the engine with a practiced hand. He was swarthy, his skin tanned and roughened by the sun, with dark, tousled hair that fell just past his ears. His face was strikingly beautiful, with chiseled features and piercing eyes that seemed to see right through me. But it was the nose ring—a small gold hoop glinting against his rugged appearance—that caught me off guard. It seemed out of place on a man like him, yet somehow, it fit perfectly, adding an unexpected edge to his allure.

He leaned forward, resting a muscled forearm on the edge of the boat as he looked me over, a slow, lazy smile spreading across his lips. "Well, well, looka wah we got here," he drawled, his voice thick with a Cajun accent that rolled off his tongue. "A city boy, lost in the swamp, messin' up his fancy shoos."

I flushed, trying to regain my composure. "Not exactly lost," I replied, though the waver in my voice betrayed me. "Just… exploring."

He chuckled, the sound low and rich, as if he found the whole situation amusing. "E'splorin' huh? Dats wah you call it?" He straightened up and offered me a hand. "Name's Beau. Beau Ducre. But folks 'round here just call me Beau."

I hesitated for a split second before taking his hand. His grip was firm, the callouses on his palm rough against my smooth skin. "Nice to meet you, Beau," I managed, trying to ignore the way my heart was pounding in my chest. "I'm…"

"Brad. I know who you are," he interrupted, his grin widening with a knowing glint in his eye.

My heart skipped a beat. How did he know my name? But before I could ask, Beau was back at the controls, steering the boat through the winding waterways with an ease that suggested he'd been doing it all his life. The swamp closed in around us, the tall grasses and drooping moss casting long shadows as the sun began its descent.

We pulled up to a small shack perched on the edge of the bayou, barely visible among the trees and overgrowth. It was a shabby thing, patched together with weathered wood and corrugated metal, looking like it had seen more than its fair share of storms. A faint smell of smoke and something earthy hung in the air, and I could hear the distant croak of a bullfrog somewhere in the distance.

"This is your place?" I asked, trying to keep the judgment out of my voice. It was a far cry from the penthouse suite I was used to, and I couldn't help but feel a twinge of discomfort at the thought of stepping inside.

Beau turned to me, that easy grin still plastered on his face as he hopped off the boat and onto the rickety wooden dock. "Yessir, dis here's home," he said, giving a casual shrug as if the shack was just another extension of himself. "She ain't much ta look at, but she keeps da rain off my head an' da gators outta my bed. 'Sides, it's all 'bout what's inside, non?"

I could barely understand him.

I hesitated for a moment, but there was no turning back now. I followed him onto the dock, trying to ignore the creak of the old wood beneath my feet.

Beau led the way to the front door, which looked like it was salvaged from a scrapyard and hastily nailed into place. He pushed it open with a creak, revealing a dimly lit interior that smelled faintly of wood smoke and herbs. It was shabby chic inside, with walls lined with shelves crammed full of jars, books, and strange trinkets that I couldn't even begin to identify. A small wood-burning stove sat in the corner, with a cast-iron pot bubbling away on top, filling the room with a savory aroma.

"C'mon in," Beau said, motioning me inside. "Ain't gonna bite ya, non." He chuckled softly as he noticed my hesitation. "Less ya ask me to, dat is."

I stepped across the threshold, trying to adjust to the sudden change in atmosphere. The shack was cramped and cluttered, a far cry from the sleek, minimalist-styled spaces I was accustomed to, but it had a strange, cozy warmth to it. Beau seemed at ease here, moving around the space with the confidence of knowing every inch of it.

He disappeared into another room for a moment and returned with a pair of dry socks and a rag. "Here," he said, handing them to me. They were thick, warm woolen socks. "Get ya feet dry, an' I'll see what I can do 'bout dem fancy shoes a'yours."

I took the socks and rag, grateful for the dry warmth, even if the socks themselves were a far cry from my usual cotton blends. As I peeled off my wet socks and slid on the new ones, I couldn't help but feel a mix of frustration and curiosity. What the hell was I doing here, in this backwater bayou, with a man who seemed more myth than reality?

"So," I started, trying to mask my skepticism, "how'd you know who I am?"

Beau glanced up from where he was kneeling by the stove, carefully placing my Prada shoes near the heat to dry. "Ain't hard ta figure out," his accent as thick as the bayou air. "Dis place? It's where folks end up when dey need lil' somethin' more den wha da city can give 'em. An' you? You got 'dat look, like you ain't quite sure why ya here, but sumptin' brought ya all da same."

I blinked a few times, my ears trying to make sense of the words he threw at me.

Nothing.

"Huh?" I grunted.

"Dis your fantasy," he said, his inflection almost kid-like.

I scoffed, leaning back against the wall, the rough wood scratching my back. "This is not my fantasy," I said, more to myself than to him. "If anything, this is a nightmare."

Beau just smiled, that easy, knowing grin that

suggested he knew more than he was letting on. "Maybe dat's da point," he hissed softly. "Maybe it's 'bout findin' what ya need, even if it ain't wha ya want."

I opened my mouth to argue, to dismiss the words as the ramblings of a man who'd spent too much time alone in the swamp, but something stopped me. Another idea wormed its way into my mind, one that felt more comfortable, more in line with how I saw the world. Maybe I was here to help Beau—show him a few things from the city. After all, who better to introduce him to a different way of life than someone who'd perfected it?

"Maybe," I said slowly, testing the idea as I spoke, "maybe I'm here to help you."

Beau's eyes sparkled with amusement as he stood up, dusting off his hands. "Help me, huh?" he repeated, his tone teasing and half curious. "An' how ya figger dat?"

I straightened up, feeling a flicker of my old confidence returning. "Maybe you need a little refinement," I said, my voice firming up. "A little lesson in living... upscale."

Beau let out a deep, rich laugh that filled the small shack. "Well now, ain't dat a thing,""he said, shaking his head with a grin. "Go on, Brad, give it a shot. Teach me all 'bout bein' a proper city gentleman."

I smirked, giggling a little as I thought about how Beau would be my "pretty woman." This could be fun, but where to even start with this guy? I looked him up and down. "Perhaps we start with a shower."

"I like where dis is goin'," he said, and unbuttoned his overalls, letting them sink to the floor with a thud. Beau stood there in all his glory, exposed to me.

My jaw dropped.

3

"You gonna join me, then?" Beau asked, tilting his head toward the bathroom.

I looked around the shack, feeling the rough edges of the room press in on me, then back at Beau. He stood there with easy confidence, as if the idea of sharing a shower was the most natural thing in the world.

"Ain't nobody here but us," Beau said, winking at me. "You can help me get nice and clean fo' ya."

My heart pounded in my chest, the suggestion hanging heavy in the air between us. The room was already filled with the humid warmth of the shower, and the idea of stripping off my clothes, letting the water wash away the swamp, was becoming more tempting by the second.

Without another word, I began to unbutton my shirt, each movement deliberate as I tried to keep my composure. Beau watched me with an intensity that sent a bolt of electricity through me. His eyes followed my every move as I shrugged out of my shirt and folded it neatly on the chair by the sink. I slipped off my trousers next, laying them gently beside the shirt, and then my underwear, the cool air brushing against my skin as I stood there, exposed and vulnerable in the dim light of the bathroom.

Beau, still wearing nothing, stood there with his muscular frame adorned with sun-kissed rough skin, slick with sweat and dirt. He possessed a rugged, untamed beauty that felt as natural and raw as the wildness of the swamp surrounding us.

I stepped closer, the heat from his body mixing with the steam in the air, and we stepped into the shower. I reached for the bar of soap resting in the basket that hung from the showerhead. Beau turned toward the shower, stepping under the spray of the water with a satisfied sigh as the warm water cascaded over his broad shoulders, washing away the grime and much of the bayou.

I followed him, the water hitting my skin like a hot embrace as I lathered the soap between my hands, creating a rich, fragrant lather that filled the small space with the scent of fresh herbs and cedarwood. Beau turned to face me, his dark eyes gleaming with desire as he took a step closer, his heat melding with mine under the spray.

Slowly, I reached up and began to work the lather across his chest, my hands gliding over his rough skin, feeling the hardness of his muscles beneath my fingers. Beau closed his eyes, a low hum of pleasure escaping his lips as I moved the soap in slow, deliberate circles, rubbing away the dirt and sweat, leaving only clean, slick skin in its place.

I continued down his torso, my touch firm yet gentle, every movement deliberate, every inch of him becoming more intoxicating as I explored the contours of his body. The water mixed with the soap, creating trails of suds that rolled down his chest, over his abs, and down his legs, pooling at his feet in a swirl of soap and dirt.

I took a step back to look at him. Beau was lean but strong, his muscles looked carved by nature rather than by a gym. His body was adorned with random tattoos, clearly impulsive choices, yet on him, they were endearing.

Beau's hands found my waist, pulling me closer until our bodies were pressed together, his wet skin against mine sending a jolt of pleasure through me. He leaned in, his breath against my ear as he muttered, "Ya got a good touch, cher."

I could feel his hands moving, sliding down my back, the roughness of his palms contrasting with the smoothness of the water-slicked soap. He took the soap from my hands and worked it between his own before slowly running them across my chest, mirroring the motions I had just made on him. The feeling was electric, every touch sending sparks of pleasure through my body as he took his time, savoring every inch of me.

The scent of the soap mingled with the steam, filling my senses with the fresh, earthy aroma of cedar and pine. I could feel the tension draining from my body as Beau's hands moved lower, tracing the lines of my hips, the curves of my thighs, until he was exploring every part of me.

Beau stepped back into the water and pulled me along to warm us back up. After a thorough rinse, we separated again, and he motioned toward the soap. "You gonna help me soap up, or I gotta do dat myself?" he said with a wink.

I could only nod as I reached out with my soapy hands and continued their sensual exploration of his body. The water cascading along his torso, following the contours of his muscles, washed away everything but the heat of the moment. Every touch, every movement, was slow and gentle, building a tension between us that felt like it could snap at any moment.

I lathered up more soap and placed my hands back on his sides. I worked up along his torso, feeling the softer, more sensitive skin. Beau let out a low moan as I moved my way up his sides. He raised his arms above his head, and I moved into his pits.

Beau closed his eyes, enjoying wash. He threw his head back and let out another low moan, almost a growl. His reaction sent a thrill through me, the vulnerability making my pulse quicken. The water poured over us, amplifying the sensation of my hands gliding over his skin, the soap making every movement smooth and deliberate. Beau's muscles flexed under my touch, his body responding to every gentle press of my fingers.

I moved up along his arms, tracing the sinewy lines, feeling the strength beneath the surface. I worked over his shoulders, down the curves of his biceps, before circling back to his chest.

Beau's breath hitched, his body leaning into my touch. His skin was warm under my fingers, and the combination of the steam and the heat radiating between us made the space feel smaller, more enclosed, as if we were the only two people in the world. His chest rose and fell with his deep, steady breaths, each one punctuated by a low, growling moan that sent shivers down my spine.

I continued to explore him, letting my hands slide lower, tracing the defined lines of his abs, feeling the way his muscles tensed and relaxed beneath my touch. He lowered his arms, bringing his hands to rest on my shoulders, his grip firm but gentle as he guided me lower, the water washing over my head.

His hands moved to cup my face, tilting my head back slightly so that I was staring up at him again. There was a raw intensity in his gaze, a mixture of desire and something deeper, something that felt like understanding or even acceptance. Without a word, he leaned over, his lips capturing mine in a slow, sensual kiss, the kind that makes you forget where you are, lost in the feeling of the moment.

The kiss deepened, his tongue sliding against mine in a dance that matched the slow rhythm we'd built between us. We broke the kiss, and he stood back up. My eyes followed his body from his nose ring, down his strong torso, and landing on his girthy cock.

Beau's cock was a vision of perfection. His girth, length, and veiny texture made my mouth water. I looked back up at him.

"It's okay to look an' touch, cher," he said, giving me a coy wink.

I reached out with my freshly soaped hands and grasped him. I wrapped my hand around the middle of his shaft and worked my way to the base, letting the soap slick my hand across him. Then, I stroked back toward his tip, letting the soap coat his entire length. On my second stroke inward, I applied more pressure to my grip.

Beau let out another one of his deep moans. Keeping my pressure steady, I stroked out to the tip of his cock again, gently tugging at his foreskin. Applying a little more pressure, I slicked my fist back down his shaft to the base. I could feel him swell and harden in my palm.

Beau murmured something under his breath, but I didn't catch it. I kept going, his engorged shaft in my hand, stroking him down and back up again, faster and faster. His back arched, and his hips thrust into my fist. Faster and faster, I stroked him, feeling him shift and squirm under my touch.

With a loud, primal groan, he came, his load shooting all over my face. I instinctively closed my eyes, feeling the hot, sticky fluid drip down. Before I could react, I heard Beau say, "Lemme get dat fo' ya."

Beau bent down and licked his mess off my face. I watched him through one open eye as he lapped up his cream, then swallowed it down. I was stunned, my jaw slack, and then I was shocked again by how turned on I was. He reached down, stuck his hands under my arms, and lifted me to my feet as if I weighed nothing. He pulled me back into the running water to rinse my face. I felt his rough yet gentle hands washing me clean.

He pulled my face close to his and kissed me once again. When we finally broke apart, both of us were breathless, our foreheads resting together as the water, still warm, continued to rain down on us. Beau's lips brushed my cheek, his voice a low, gravelly whisper. "Dat's da best clean I ever had, cher," he said softly, his voice laced with satisfaction.

I was too stunned to speak, but I couldn't help the smile that tugged at my lips—a mix of satisfaction and something deeper, something more complicated that I wasn't ready to name yet.

Finding my voice, I managed to say, "I'm glad I could help."

We stood there for a moment longer, grounding ourselves in the reality of the moment, even though it felt like something out of a dream. Eventually, Beau reached for the shower controls, turning the water off with a final, satisfying hiss. The room fell quiet, the only sound our breathing, the space still filled with steam and the lingering scent of soap.

"So, what's da next step in becomin' a refined gentleman?" Beau asked, a cocky grin spreading across his face.

4

Beau stepped out of the shower first, grabbing a towel and tossing it to me before wrapping another around his waist. His easy grin was back, though there was something softer, more open in his eyes now. "Reckon I'm clean enough for ya now, cher?" he said, his accent as thick as ever.

"Why do you keep calling me cher?" I asked, hoping to convey the playful charm in my heart.

"It's short for *mon cheri*. It's Creole for *my dear*. It's a term of endearment," he explained. "Oh, *shabbow*! Look at me, using endearment—like a fancy five-dollar word."

Beau leaned in and gave me a quick kiss on the

mouth. "I think it's working after all…," he said and danced out of the bathroom.

I nodded, still processing everything that had just happened, the mix of emotions swirling inside me. As I dried off and followed him, I couldn't shake the feeling that something had shifted between us. Something I hadn't expected but couldn't ignore.

As I stepped out of the bathroom, towel wrapped around my waist, I glanced down at my bare feet, already missing the polished leather of my Prada shoes. "I wish I had my clothes," I muttered, half to myself.

Beau, now in the middle of the room, looked up with a twinkle in his eye. "Don't worry 'bout dat, cher. Look over by da door. Reckon ya might find somethin' familiar."

Curious, I walked over to the door and, to my surprise, found a suitcase—my suitcase—propped up against the wall. Relief washed over me as I saw my clothes packed neatly inside, along with a few of my favorite accessories. I pulled out a crisp shirt and a pair of tailored trousers, feeling more like myself already.

But as I held my clothes in my hands, another idea struck me. I glanced over at Beau, who was watching me with that easy grin of his, and a thought began to take shape—half-ridiculous, half-intriguing.

"Hey Beau," I said softly, holding up the shirt. "I think you're ready for step two. How would you feel about trying on some of these?"

He raised an eyebrow, clearly amused by the suggestion. "You want me to put on some o' yer fancy city clothes? Ain't never worn nothin' like dat before."

"Exactly," I replied, my excitement growing. "Come on, let's see how you look in something a little different."

"Alright," he leapt forward, dropping his towel. "Why not? Can't hurt ta try."

I looked away and handed him the shirt.

"You're awfully shy for a fella who just had my slick all over your face a few minutes ago," Beau teased. "It's okay to look, cher. It's all yours."

I watched as he slipped on the shirt, the crisp white fabric a stark contrast against his dark skin. He fumbled with the buttons for a moment with his calloused fingers. Next came the underwear. I handed him a sexy, black brief-style pair, and he slipped them on with ease.

I handed him the next article of clothing—the

trousers. He slid into them easily, though they were clearly a new experience for him.

"Dis feels strange," he admitted, looking down at himself. "Ain't never worn no pants dat fit so… snug."

I chuckled, stepping closer to adjust the collar of his shirt, my fingers brushing against the warm skin of his neck. "You'll get used to it. Besides, you look great."

And he did.

I gave him a look up and down, gently tousling his messy hair until it lay nicely. He looked really sexy in my clothes, but at the same time, something about the outfit seemed off. I couldn't put my finger on it.

Beau glanced at himself in the small, cracked mirror by the door, his expression shifting from mild discomfort to something closer to awe. "Well, I'll be," he murmured, his voice almost reverent. "Ain't never seen myself lookin' like dis before, non."

He turned to face me, his eyes meeting mine, full of vulnerability and pride. "Ya really think I look good in dis, Brad?"

I nodded, unable to keep the smile off my face. "You look incredible, Beau. Like you were made for this."

He grinned and rolled his shoulders back as if trying to settle into the new clothes. "Ain't sure 'bout dat, but I gotta admit, it's nice. Feels... different."

We spent the next few minutes with Beau trying on more of my clothes, each outfit drawing out laughter from both of us. He slipped into a tailored jacket, admiring the way it hugged his broad shoulders, then tried on a pair of my designer jeans, surprised by how comfortable they were despite their fitted cut.

There was something endearing about the way he studied himself in the mirror, as if seeing a different side of himself for the first time.

He adjusted a silk tie around his neck, fumbling with the unfamiliar knot. I stepped in to help, our hands brushing as I guided him through the process. "It's all in the wrist. Over, under, and through," I explained, showing him how to loop the tie just right.

Beau watched me with a soft smile, his eyes twinkling with something that felt like gratitude. "Ain't never thought I'd be wearin' somethin' like dis, but I gotta say, I like it."

We stood there, side by side, both of us dressed in clothes that reflected who I was, yet somehow made Beau look like he'd been wearing them all his life. The laughter, the teasing, the shared glances— all felt like a breath of fresh air.

Beau caught my eye, a playful glint back in his gaze. "Reckon we oughta go show off dis new look, don't ya think, cher?"

I laughed, feeling lighter than I had in a long time. "Absolutely. Let's go turn some heads."

And with that, we headed for the door, a pair of unlikely companions, dressed to the nines and ready for the night.

The path leading back to town was lined with towering cypress trees, their roots twisting in and out of the murky water that lapped at the edges of the trail. The setting sun cast a warm, golden hue over everything, making the world feel soft and dreamlike.

Beau walked beside me, his usual swagger now replaced with a shy excitement as he tugged at the cuffs of his borrowed jacket. He looked over at me with that mischievous grin I was starting to recognize as his trademark. "So, cher, where we headin'? You gonna show me how da other half lives?"

I laughed, shaking my head. "Something like that. I figure we should find a place to eat, give those clothes a proper outing."

He chuckled, his hand brushing mine as we walked. "Long as I'm wit' you, I don' care where we gonna end up. 'Sides, gotta admit, dis whole fancy getup makes me feel like a million bucks."

The rough, wild edges of the bayou gave way to charming streets lined with old brick buildings, their windows glowing with soft lights. It was a picturesque scene, a far cry from the frantic pace of the city, but there was something undeniably appealing about it.

I scanned the street, looking for a place that felt just right. That's when I saw a small upscale restaurant tucked between two quaint shops, its name elegantly displayed in gold lettering above the door. "Le Mistral," it read, promising a mix of French elegance and Southern charm.

"This looks perfect," I said, nodding towards the entrance.

Beau followed my gaze, his eyes widening as he took in the sight. "Well, I'll be," he murmured, clearly awed. "Ain't never been to no place like dis before."

"First time for everything," I said with a smile, pushing the door open and gesturing for him to step inside.

The interior was just as refined as I had hoped.

Le Mistral was dimly lit with soft, amber lighting that reflected off the polished wood floors and white tablecloths. The scent of freshly baked bread and rich sauces filled the air, mingling with the low hum of conversation. Beau hesitated at the entrance, his eyes darting around as if unsure whether he belonged in such a place.

But I gave him a reassuring nudge, leading him to a table near the window. "You're going to love this," I promised, pulling out a chair for him before taking a seat across the table.

As we settled in, a waiter approached with a smile, handing us each a menu. Beau stared at his, brow furrowed as he tried to decipher the elegant script and unfamiliar dish names. "Don't know none of dis," he admitted with a sheepish grin.

"Let's make a deal," I suggested, leaning in conspiratorially. "I'll order for you, and you can order for me. That way, we both get to try something new."

Beau's eyes lit up, his smile returning full force. "Now dat's a plan I can get behind." He glanced at the menu again, then back at me, clearly excited for the challenge. "Alright, cher. Let's see what fancy foods you think I'll like."

I scanned the menu, my eyes landing on a dish

that I knew would be perfect for him—something rich, flavorful, and undeniably sophisticated. "How about the pan-seared duck breast with a port wine reduction, served alongside truffle-infused pommes purée and a medley of haricots verts and heirloom carrots?"

Beau's eyes widened. "I only understood da words duck and carrots, but alright."

He studied the menu with a seriousness that was both endearing and amusing, his lips moving slightly as he sounded out the names of the dishes. After a moment, his face lit up with a grin. "Alright, Brad. How 'bout we go wit' somethin' a lil' closer to home. How you feel 'bout some gumbo and boudin balls?"

I couldn't help but laugh; I didn't understand what he was getting for me either. "Sounds perfect."

When the waiter returned, we placed our orders, exchanging amused glances as we handed over the menus. As we waited for our food, Beau's eyes kept wandering around the restaurant, taking in every detail as if he were afraid he might miss something. There was a sense of wonder in his gaze that made me see him through new eyes.

"So, dis what y'all do in da city?" he asked, leaning back in his chair. "Dress up all fancy-like, go to places like dis, eat food wit' names ya can hardly pronounce?"

"Pretty much," I replied with a chuckle. "It's about the experience, I guess. But honestly, it's more fun being here… with you."

Beau flashed me that lopsided grin again, his hand resting on the table just inches from mine. "I'm glad I'm here wit' you."

Our food arrived, and we both laughed as we dug into our unfamiliar dishes, each of us trying to make sense of the new flavors and textures. Beau's eyes nearly rolled back in his head as he tasted his duck. "*Shabbow!*" he exclaimed. "Dis… dis is somethin' else."

Meanwhile, I found myself pleasantly surprised by the gumbo and boudin balls—the flavors bold and comforting, a far cry from the usual fare I was accustomed to. We shared bites of each other's meals, laughing as we compared notes and joked about how perfect the evening was turning out to be.

By the time we finished, both of us were full and happy, the atmosphere between us relaxed and warm. We paid the bill and stepped back into the cool night air, Beau slipping his hand into mine as we walked back.

"Dat was somethin' else, cher," he said, low and content. "Never thought I'd enjoy a place like dat, but I gotta admit, it might have been the company."

"I'm glad you liked it," I replied, giving his hand a gentle squeeze. "You too are something else. Thank you for sharing that with me."

Beau leaned in and planted a quick kiss on my cheek. "Yer a sweet talker, Brad. But I ain't complainin'."

The walk back to Beau's place was filled with easy conversation and laughter. As we stepped inside his place, the familiar scent of wood smoke and herbs greeted us, grounding us back to each other.

Beau slipped off his jacket, hanging it on a hook by the door, and turned to me with a smile that made my heart skip a beat. "Reckon it's time ta get comfy again, don't ya think?"

I nodded, following his lead as we both began to shed the fancy clothes.

5

Beau pulled me close, his arms wrapping around me in a warm, reassuring embrace. We locked eyes, and I couldn't resist any longer—I pulled him to me, pressing a passionate kiss onto his lips.

Beau responded with an intensity that took my breath away. His lips were firm yet soft against mine, moving in perfect sync as the heat between us began to build. The warmth of his skin seeped into mine, his hand roaming up and down my back, pulling me closer until there wasn't an inch of space left between us.

As our tongues met, sliding together in a slow, deliberate dance, a surge of desire made my head spin. My hands found their way to the buttons of my shirt he was wearing. I unbuttoned one and slipped a finger beneath the fabric, exploring the hard planes of his chest. His skin was warm and despite its roughness, his muscles tensed under my touch. I ran my hands over the ridges of his abs, savoring the feeling of his body responding to me.

I unbuttoned the rest of his shirt, and Beau let out a low, throaty moan as I pulled it from his arms, breaking the kiss just long enough to tug it off and toss it aside. His eyes darkened with desire as he pulled me back to him, his lips crashing against mine with renewed fervor. His hands were everywhere—tangling in my hair, gripping my shoulders, sliding down to my waist as he pressed me against him.

My own shirt was gone in an instant, lost somewhere in the flurry of movement as Beau's hands continued their exploration. He traced the lines of my chest, his fingers brushing over my nipples, sending jolts of pleasure through me. I gasped against his mouth, the sound swallowed by a kiss as his tongue explored every inch of my mouth with a hunger that matched my own.

We stumbled back toward the bed, our lips never breaking apart as we moved together, shedding the last remnants of clothing in a haze of heated passion. My pants fell to the floor, quickly followed by Beau's, and then we were skin to skin, his warm body pressed against mine, his erection brushing against my thigh as we finally collapsed onto the bed.

Beau hovered over me, his hands braced on either side of my head as he looked down at me, his eyes blazing with an intensity that made my heart race. He leaned down, his lips trailing hot, open-mouthed kisses along my jaw, down to my neck, sucking and nipping at the sensitive skin until I was arching up against him, desperate for more.

My hands roamed over his back, tracing the contours of his muscles, feeling them ripple beneath my touch as he continued to explore my body with his mouth. He kissed his way down my chest, his tongue flicking out to tease my nipples, making me gasp and writhe beneath him. Every touch, every kiss, sent waves of pleasure coursing through me, the tension between us building to a fever pitch.

I ran my fingers through his hair, gripping it tightly as he moved lower, his lips brushing over my abdomen. I jumped slightly at the cold touch of his golden nose ring. The anticipation was almost unbearable, making my entire body ache for him.

Beau seemed to sense it, his hands sliding down

to my hips as he looked up at me, a wicked grin spreading across his face. "Ya taste so good, cher. Can't get enough of ya."

I tugged him back up, capturing his lips in another searing kiss, the need between us growing with every passing second. His hands explored every inch of my body, his touch tender yet demanding, driving me to the edge without pushing me over.

We rolled together on the bed, our bodies tangled in a heated embrace, kissing, touching, exploring—every moment building higher and higher. The walls echoed our heavy breathing, the scent of our arousal filling the air as we continued to stoke the fire between us.

Beau's lips found mine again, his kiss softer this time, more languid as he pressed his body against mine, our erections brushing together, sending a shudder of pleasure through me. His hands cupped my face, his thumb brushing over my cheek as he pulled back just enough to look into my eyes.

"Yer somethin' else, Brad," he said, his voice thick with emotion. "Ain't never felt like dis before."

I smiled up at him, my heart swelling with emotions. "Me either," I admitted quietly.

We stayed like that for a moment, just holding

each other, our breathing slowing as the intensity of the moment settled into something deeper. Beau's hands stroked my sides, his touch soothing, grounding me in the reality of what was happening between us.

Beau resumed his exploration, his kisses trailing lower and lower. He hovered, drawing gentle circles with his tongue around my navel. His chest hovered above my cock, brushing it gently with the tufts of his chest hair. He moved down to my cock and kissed the tip.

In one quick movement, he took all of me into his mouth. Beau's sudden movement sent a shock-wave through me, my breath catching as the warmth of his mouth enveloped me completely. The contrast between his earlier tender touches and the sudden, overwhelming sensation left me gasping, my hands instinctively gripping the sheets beneath me.

He paused for a moment, letting me feel the fullness of the moment. His tongue pressed against my dick, swirling in slow, deliberate motions that made my head spin. The sensation was almost too much, but before I could catch my breath, he began to move again, his mouth sliding up and down my length with a tempo that was both torturously slow and incredibly intense.

His hands gripped my hips, holding me steady as he worked, his mouth creating a delicious friction that made it impossible to think, to do anything but feel. The way he moved was unhurried, as if he was savoring every second, every reaction he pulled from me. And gods above, he was pulling reactions from me.

My hips bucked instinctively, seeking more of the sensation he was delivering, but Beau held me firm, his control over the situation only adding to the heat building inside me. The gentle scrape of his stubbled jaw against my skin, the soft sounds of his mouth on me, and the pressure of his hands on my hips combined into an inundating wave of ecstasy that had me teetering on the edge.

Beau pulled back slightly, his tongue teasing the sensitive underside of my cock before taking me in again, his pace quickening, the suction of his mouth increasing. I could feel the heat in my middle building, coiling tighter and tighter with every movement, every flick of his tongue, every slide of his lips.

My hands moved from the sheets to his hair, fingers tangling in his soft strands. The need inside me grew with every passing second. I was close—so close—and Beau knew it. My fingers tightened in his hair.

But then, just as I was about to tip over the edge, Beau pulled back, releasing me from his mouth. I gasped, the sudden loss leaving me heaving, my entire body trembling for release.

He looked up at me, that devilish grin on his face, his eyes dark with desire. "Not yet, cher," he said, his Cajun drawl driving me wild. "Ain't done suckin' at ya yet."

With that, he began his descent again, his mouth and hands moving in tandem as he kissed his way back up my body, tracing the lines of my hips, my stomach, the curves of my chest. Each touch was electrifying, heightening my senses, accentuated by the feeling of his erection brushing against me as he made his way up.

As Beau's mouth found mine again, he kissed me with a hunger that was evident in the hard length pressing into me. He laid down, pressing his weight against me, our bodies slick with sweat and desire. His hands roamed my body, as if he were committing it to memory, and I responded in kind. The need inside me was almost unbearable now, every nerve ending alive with the anticipation of what was to come.

"Ya feel good, Brad," he murmured. "Real good. You want me ta finish ya off?"

I nodded, too lost in the sensation to form coherent words, and he returned to my middle. His lips curled around my cock, taking me further down his throat than before. As the tip of my cock met the back of his throat, he only took me deeper. The tightness of his throat took my breath away. He held it for a few seconds and then began thrusting, deep, wet, and tight into his mouth.

Quicker and with growing urgency, he moved my cock in and out of his mouth. Each thrust sent a jolt through my body. The pressure was building with every second, every expert flick of his tongue, and every deep, wet pull of his lips. My body shook, my muscles tensed as the waves of pleasure rolled over me, growing stronger. Beau's eyes met mine, his mouth full of me. He increased the pace, his mouth working with practiced skill.

The tightness in my abdomen grew unbearable. "Beau," I gasped, "I'm close, so close."

He didn't slow down, didn't let up for even a second. If anything, he only intensified his efforts, his mouth moving faster, his throat tightening around me as he pushed me closer to the brink. The pressure inside me built to a crescendo, my entire body trembling as I felt the orgasm rising, unstoppable.

And then, with one final thrust, I was there, exploding into his mouth with a force that left me quaking, my vision going white as the orgasm consumed me. Beau took it all, his throat working around me, swallowing every last drop as I pulsed inside his mouth.

He held me there, his mouth still wrapped around me, milking every bit of my release until I was completely spent. Finally, he pulled back, his lips releasing me with a soft, wet sound, and looked up at me with a satisfied grin, his lips glistening.

I collapsed back against the pillows, my chest heaving as I tried to catch my breath, my mind still reeling from the aftershocks. Beau crawled up beside me, his hand resting on my chest, his touch grounding me as I slowly came back to myself.

"Ya taste even better than I thought," he said, his voice low and rough. He leaned in, pressing a gentle kiss to my lips, and I could taste myself on him, the lingering sweetness of my release mingling with the saltiness of his skin.

I wrapped my arms around him, pulling him

close, feeling his body against mine, the connection between us stronger than ever. We lay there together, tangled in each other's arms, the room filled with the sound of our breathing as we basked in the afterglow, content and utterly spent.

For a moment, neither of us spoke, simply enjoying the quiet intimacy that had settled between us. Beau's fingers traced lazy patterns on my chest, his touch soothing and tender. I felt a deep sense of peace, of belonging, like everything in that moment was exactly as it should be.

"Yer somethin' else, Brad," Beau murmured, his voice filled with emotion. "Ain't never felt this way before."

I looked into his eyes, seeing the vulnerability there, and my heart swelled with affection. "Me neither, Beau. Me neither." We stayed like that, holding each other close, letting the world outside fade away.

6

I woke to the soft glow of morning light filtering through the gaps in the curtains of Beau's bedroom. I was still wrapped in Beau's embrace, his arms draped possessively over my waist. His chest pressed against my back, the steady rise and fall of his breathing in sync with mine.

For a moment, I didn't move, savoring the quiet intimacy of the moment. The feel of his body, the comforting weight of his arms, the way his breath tickled the back of my neck—it all felt so right. It was a far cry from the sterile mornings in my penthouse, where the only sounds were the distant hum of the city and the occasional buzz of my phone. Here, in this little place on the edge of the bayou, the world felt slower, softer, and infinitely more real.

I realized this was the first time I had reflected on my life in New York since arriving here. The relentless pace, the constant push to succeed, to be better, faster, more successful—it was as if I had been trapped in a race with no finish line. I had pushed myself so hard because I thought that was what it meant to be alive, to be valuable. But the truth was, I was running myself into the ground, consumed by the need to prove something—to the world, but mostly to myself. The stress had become a constant companion, an unyielding pressure that drove me forward but also crushed me under its weight. Here, in the quiet of the bayou, I could finally see how much it had taken from me—the joy, the peace, the ability to simply be without the nagging voice in the back of my mind telling me I wasn't enough.

I shifted slightly, turning in his arms so I could see his face. Beau was still asleep, his features relaxed, a small smile playing on his lips as if he were dreaming of something pleasant. I hoped he was. The morning light made his skin glow, high-lighting the angles of his face, the stubble on his jaw, and the tousled waves of his hair. He looked peaceful, content, and in that moment, I couldn't help but feel a rush of affection for this man.

I reached up, touching him gently on his fore-head, my fingers lingering on his skin, marveling at how he felt beneath my touch. Beau stirred slightly, his eyes fluttering open, and when they met mine, my heart skipped a beat.

"Mornin', cher," he murmured, his voice husky with sleep. He pulled me closer, nuzzling his face into the crook of my neck. "Ya sleep good?"

"Better than I have in a long time," I admit-ted, my fingers tracing lazy circles on his back. "You?"

He chuckled softly, the sound vibrating against my chest. "Ain't never woke up feelin' dis good before. Must be 'cause I got ya here wit' me."

We lay there for a while, wrapped in each other's arms, content to let the world outside pass us by. Eventually, Beau shifted, propping himself up on one elbow as he looked down at me with his signa-ture grin. "Ya know, I been thinkin'," he began, trailing his fingers down my side. "How 'bout I take ya out into the bayou today? Show ya a lil' more 'bout my world."

I raised an eyebrow, curious but also slightly wary. "Okay…"

Beau chuckled, giving me a wink as he climbed out of bed and began pulling on his clothes. "Don't worry, cher. I'll protect ya. Now, git dressed. We got us an adventure ta start."

I pulled on my clothes with a mix of anticipation and nerves. By the time we were both dressed, the sun filtered through the windows as if blessing the day ahead.

We stepped outside, the humid air wrapping around us in an embrace. Beau led the way, his hand slipping into mine as we made our way through the dense foliage, the ground soft and spongy beneath our feet. The bayou was alive with sound and color, the morning light glinting off the water, making it sparkle like a thousand diamonds.

As we climbed aboard his boat, I couldn't help but feel a mix of excitement and nervousness. The boat was small and rustic, much like everything else about Beau's life here, but it felt sturdy underfoot. Beau handed me a life jacket, which I accepted with a smile, though he didn't put one on himself. "You're not wearing one?" I asked, raising an eyebrow.

"Nah, I been on dis water all my life, cher. I trust it, an' it trusts me," he replied with a wink, his voice brimming with confidence. "But don't you worry. I'll keep ya safe."

With that, we pushed off from the shore, the

boat's engine sputtering to life as Beau expertly guided us through the winding waterways of the bayou. The morning mist hung low over the water, adding a mystical quality to the scenery. The thick canopy of trees overhead filtered the sunlight, casting dappled shadows on the surface of the water, which shimmered like liquid gold.

As we glided deeper into the bayou, Beau began pointing out various plants and animals with the enthusiasm of someone sharing a deeply cherished secret. "See dat over dere?" he said, nodding toward a cluster of low-hanging branches draped with moss. "Dat's Spanish moss. It don't harm the trees, just hangs out like a lazy ol' ghost. My grand-mère used ta say it was the hair of spirits who couldn't move on."

I leaned in closer, intrigued by the way the moss swayed gently in the breeze. "It's beautiful," I murmured, captivated by the ethereal quality of the landscape. "Your grandmother sounds like she had some interesting stories."

"Oh, she did, cher," Beau replied with a grin. "She was full of 'em. She used ta tell me stories 'bout dis place, how the bayou's alive, breathin' and feelin' just like you an' me. Said if you listen close enough, you can hear its heart beatin'."

I looked out at the water, suddenly aware of the symphony of sounds around us—the distant croak of frogs, the rustling of leaves, the soft lapping of water against the boat. It did feel alive, vibrant with a life force that was palpable. "Do you believe that?" I asked, turning back to Beau.

He paused for a moment, his eyes scanning the horizon. "I do," he said softly, his voice tinged with reverence. "Dis place… it's in my blood. I feel it here," he placed a hand over his heart. "Every time I step out into the bayou, I feel like I'm comin' home."

His words struck a chord in me, and I found myself in awe of his connection to this place. It was a love so deep and intrinsic that it defined him, and in that moment, I realized how much I admired him for it. "You're really passionate about this place, aren't you?" I said, more a statement than a question.

Beau smiled, a soft, almost shy expression that made my heart skip a beat. "Yeah, I reckon I am. Dis place raised me, taught me everythin' I know. It's wild an' untamed, but it's also home. I can't imagine livin' anywhere else."

We continued our journey, and Beau's voice took on a storytelling cadence as he shared more about the bayou. "See dat tree over dere? Dat's a cypress. They say cypress trees are the oldest livin' things in the bayou. Some of 'em been 'round for hundreds of years. Grandmère used ta say they were the guardians of the bayou, watchin' over everythin' that happens here."

I looked at the towering cypress trees with newfound respect, their gnarled roots twisting in and out of the water like ancient, wise sentinels. "It must be amazing, growing up surrounded by all this," I said, feeling a pang of envy for the peace and beauty of his world.

"It is," Beau agreed, his eyes sparkling with pride. "But it ain't always easy. The bayou's beautiful, sure, but it's also dangerous. Gotta respect it, or it'll remind ya who's really in charge."

"Like with the gators?" I asked, remembering the stories I'd heard about alligators lurking in the murky waters.

"Exactly," Beau said with a nod. "Gators, snakes, even the weather—out here, ya gotta be ready for anythin'. But dat's part of the beauty, too. Keeps ya on yer toes, makes ya appreciate what ya got."

After a while, we reached a small clearing where the water was calm and still, the only movement the gentle ripples caused by our boat. Beau cut the engine, and the sudden quiet felt profound, like we had entered a sacred space. He knelt by the water's edge, his movements slow and deliberate as he scanned the surface with a practiced eye.

"Now, ya gotta be real quiet, cher," he whispered, his voice low and serious. "Gators are real quick, but I'm quicker. Jus' follow my lead."

"A gator? Are you serious?" I whispered back, my heart rate spiking at the thought.

"Serious as a heart attack," he replied, grinning widely, a hint of mischief in his eyes. "But don't ya worry none, ain't no danger. I'll be right dere wit' ya. Now be quiet."

I swallowed hard, trying to calm the nerves that fluttered in my stomach. Beau's confidence was reassuring, but the idea of coming face-to-face with an alligator still sent a thrill of fear through me. I watched him move with a quiet grace that belied his usual easy-going nature, his focus entirely on the water.

For a few tense moments, nothing happened. The water was still, the bayou eerily silent as if holding its breath. Then, I saw it—a small gator, barely two feet long, gliding just beneath the surface. Its movements were smooth, almost lazy, but there was something undeniably predatory about the way it cut through the water.

"There he is," Beau whispered, his voice so soft it was almost inaudible. "Now watch closely."

Before I could even blink, Beau's hand shot out like lightning, his fingers closing around the gator's snout with a speed and precision that left me breathless. He lifted the creature out of the water, holding it carefully as it thrashed in his grip, its tail whipping back and forth.

"Gotcha," he shouted, a triumphant smile spreading across his face as he turned to show me his prize. "Ain't he a beauty?"

I stared at the gator in awe, a mix of fear and fascination bubbling up inside me. "You caught it... just like that."

Beau laughed, clearly enjoying my reaction. "Jus' like dat, cher. Now, lemme show ya somethin'." He held the gator up to me, his hands steady as he guided me to touch the rough, scaly skin. "Feel dat? Dey're tougher than dey look, but dey still need respect. Ain't no harm in 'em, long as ya know how ta handle 'em."

Tentatively, I ran my fingers over the gator's skin, the texture rough and prehistoric under my touch.

There was something strangely beautiful about it, a reminder of the raw, untamed power of nature. And as I stood there, with Beau guiding my hand, I couldn't help but feel a deep sense of connection— to the gator, to the bayou, and to the man beside me.

"Ya done good, cher," Beau said softly, his eyes meeting mine with a warmth that made my heart swell. "Reckon yer a natural."

I smiled, feeling a rush of pride and affection. "Maybe I am," I replied, my voice soft and cracking slightly.

Beau released the gator back into the water, watching as it quickly disappeared beneath the surface. Then he turned to me, his hands finding their way to my waist as he pulled me close, his lips brushing against my neck.

I giggled, wrapping my arms around his neck and pressing my forehead against his. "This is absolutely incredible."

"What is?"

"This moment. This experience. You," I admitted, leaning in to kiss him.

We stood there for a moment, wrapped in each other's arms, the world around us fading away as we lost ourselves in each other's touch. Eventually,

Beau pulled back, his eyes filled with love. "C'mon, cher. Let's keep movin'."

"Do we have to?" I asked.

"What ya got in mind?" he said, raising an eyebrow at me.

I leaned forward, grabbing his face with both of my hands, and kissed him deeply. I tugged at the hem of his shirt, pulling it up over his head. My fingers ran up his chest as I held him in our kiss.

He managed to pull my shirt off, our kiss only breaking long enough for the fabric to slide past my face. Our tongues battled wildly in our mouths, urgent and needy. I could feel my erection swelling inside my jeans. I pressed myself up against him, feeling his hardness against me.

My kiss moved from his lips to his cheek, then around to his neck just below his ear. I suckled at the soft skin there before moving up to his ear. "Can I fuck you?" I whispered gently.

"I thought ya'd never ask," Beau replied, quickly stripping off his jeans and pulling his underwear down with them. My hands trembled slightly as I unbuttoned my jeans, the cool air brushing against my skin as I pushed them down, joining Beau in a state of nakedness. The sun bathed us both, mingling with the heat radiating from our bodies as I stepped closer to him, my heart pounding.

Beau reclined against the flat surface of the boat, his legs spreading slightly to make room for me as I settled between them. His hands found my hips, guiding me closer until our bodies were flush, the sensation of his skin against mine sending shivers of pleasure through me.

I looked into his gentle eyes once more and realized why I was brought here. And maybe, just maybe, I'd be brave enough to tell him.

7

Beau caught me staring at him. "What ya thinkin' 'bout?" he asked, his voice a low, teasing rumble.

"Your sexy body," I replied with a grin, leaning down to capture his lips in a hungry, deep kiss as I positioned myself at his entrance. Beau's breath hitched, his grip on my hips tightening as I began to press into him. The tightness and heat of his body drew a low groan from my throat.

The boat rocked gently with our movements, the world around us narrowing to just the two of us —the feel of his body yielding to mine, the way he gasped and moaned as I pushed deeper inside him. Beau's legs wrapped around my waist, pulling me closer as I began to move, each thrust deliberate, designed to draw out every ounce of pleasure from the moment.

"Gods, you feel so good," I whispered against his lips, my voice thick with desire. I increased the pace, the friction nearly explosive.

Beau's head fell back, his eyes fluttering shut as he let out a low, throaty moan that echoed down the bayou. "Fuck, Brad. Don't stop."

I had no intention of stopping. The feel of him, the way his body moved with mine, the sounds he made—it was all too much. I thrust deeper, harder, the boat swaying beneath us in time with our movements. The gentle breeze of the bayou did nothing to cool the heat burning between us, making the sweat drip down from my chest.

Beau's hands roamed up my arms, his fingers digging into my skin as he urged me on, his breath coming in short, ragged gasps. I could feel the tension building inside both of us, coiling tight, ready to snap.

I shifted my angle, hitting that spot inside him that made him cry out, his voice raw and desperate. "Right there," he gasped, his words almost a plea. "Fuck, Brad… right there."

I focused on that spot, driving into him with a steady, relentless rhythm that had us both on the edge. The boat rocked harder now, the sounds of the bayou drowned out by our grunts, our panting breaths, and the slap of skin on skin.

I could feel myself getting close, the pressure building to a peak. Beau came with a shout, his body shaking beneath me as he pulsed around my cock, the intensity of his orgasm triggering the start of my own. His cum shot out of him, splattering across his chest, and without thinking, I leaned down, licked up a sample of his seed with my tongue.

The taste of him pushed me over the edge. A wave of pleasure crashed over me, leaving me breathless, trembling, and lost in the sensation of being buried inside him as I released. I thrust into him one last time, deep and hard, my body shuddering as I spilled into him.

We stayed like that for a moment, our bodies still joined, our breaths mingling in the warm, humid air as the aftershocks of our releases slowly ebbed away. The boat rocked gently, the world around us gradually coming back into focus.

Beau's hands slid up my back, pulling me down to rest against his chest, my cock slowly softening as it slipped from his body. My chest felt the slickness of his cum between us, my breath still coming in soft pants. "Shabbow," he said, his voice rough and full of satisfaction. "Dat was somethin' else, cher."

I smiled, pressing a kiss to his neck, a deep sense of contentment settling over me. "Yes, it was."

We lay there on the boat, the sun warming our skin, the sounds of the bayou wrapping around us like a blanket. The intimacy of the moment, the connection we'd just shared, felt like something out of a dream.

Beau's fingers traced lazy patterns on my back as he held me close, his lips brushing against my temple in a gesture as sweet as it was reassuring. "Reckon we should head back soon," he whispered. "I kinda feel like jus' stickin' here wit' ya, but I gotta be honest. Dem skeeters gonna be comin' out full force here quick."

I laughed, closing my eyes and letting the peace of the moment wash over me. "We better get moving then."

Reluctantly, we picked up our clothing and got dressed as quickly as we could. Beau fired up the boat, and we headed back towards his shack, the engine humming as it cut through the still waters of the bayou.

As Beau guided the boat through the winding waterways, the sun began its slow descent, casting a golden glow over everything. The hum of the fan propeller filled the air, blending with the distant sounds of the swamp—a sound I was beginning to appreciate in a way I never thought possible. I watched Beau at the helm, his easy confidence, the way he seemed so at home here, and I felt a swell of emotion rising in my chest.

We reached his shack just as the last light of day was fading, the shadows stretching long and deep across the water. Beau tied the boat to the dock with practiced ease and helped me onto the wooden planks. The smell of wood smoke and damp earth greeted us as we walked inside, a sense of comfort and belonging settling over me.

Beau glanced over at me, a small smile playing on his lips as he pulled me into his arms, holding me close. "Dat was somethin', huh?"

I nodded, resting my head on his shoulder, feeling the steady beat of his heart against my chest. "Yes, it was. But there's something I need to say, Beau. Something that took me a while to realize."

He pulled back slightly, his brow furrowing in concern as he looked at me. "What's dat, cher?"

I took a deep breath, gathering my thoughts, my hands resting on his chest as I searched for the right words. "When I first got here, I thought this fantasy was all about me trying to change you—making you more like me. Bring some of the city to the bayou. But the truth is, Beau... it wasn't about changing you at all."

His expression softened. "What d'ya mean?"

"I mean, it's me who needed to change," I confessed. "I've spent so much of my life in this frantic, endless race, trying to prove myself, trying to be something... someone I thought I needed to be. But being here, with you, I've realized that what I really need is to slow down, to take it easy. I need to learn to appreciate the little things—the joy in just being, in loving freely. And yes, even touching alligators."

Beau chuckled, tightening his hands around my waist. His gaze didn't waver as he listened, the sincerity in his eyes giving me the courage to continue.

"I was so caught up in my own world, in my own expectations, that I forgot how to really live. But you've shown me that there's more to life than just chasing the next goal, the next achievement. You've taught me to find joy in the simple things, to appreciate the beauty in the world around me, and to love without holding back. And for that, Beau, I can't thank you enough."

He was silent for a moment, his eyes searching mine as he processed my words. Then, slowly, a warm, genuine grin spread across his face. He leaned down and pressed a soft, lingering kiss to my lips.

"Ya don' gotta thank me, Brad," he murmured against my mouth. "I'm jus' glad I could share all dis wit' ya. Ain't never thought I'd meet someone like ya, but now dat I have, I can't imagine it any otha way."

I smiled, my heart full as I wrapped my arms around his neck, pulling him closer. "Me neither, Beau. Me neither."

We stood there in the quiet of the shack, holding each other, our connection filling the space between us. The world outside was still and peaceful, the sounds of the bayou a gentle reminder of the place that had become my sanctuary.

Finally, Beau pulled back, his hands cupping my face as he looked at me with a serene tenderness. "I'll tell ya what, cher," he said, his voice gentle. "We got plenty mo' time ta take it easy, ta find joy in all da lil' things. But for now, how 'bout we make some supper, light a fire, and just enjoy dis night together."

I nodded, a sense of contentment washing over me. "That sounds perfect."

As we prepared dinner, lighting the fire, and settling into the simple pleasures of the evening, I soaked in the comfort of being with Beau. Later, as we sat on the couch, the flicker of the fire casting warm shadows across the room, I leaned into him, my head resting on his shoulder, and felt a deep sense of peace.

I knew this was just the beginning—of a new chapter, a new way of living for me, one filled with love, laughter, and the kind of tranquility I had been searching for all along.

The flames of the fire hypnotized me, lulling me into a peaceful sleep as the world faded into the comforting embrace of the night.

8

I blinked myself awake, disoriented, and found myself in a plain white room. The vivid memories of where I had just been lingered in my mind, and for a moment, I felt lost, caught between two worlds. As the confusion began to ebb away, reality slowly settled back in. I remembered coming to the Arcane Room, meeting Ms. Vesper, and drinking the tea that had set everything in motion.

"Take your time getting up," Ms. Vesper's voice floated softly from the door, bringing me back to the present.

I sat up slowly, the simplicity of the room starkly contrasting with the vibrant world I had just left behind. The chaise lounge was comfortable, but it paled in comparison to the warmth of Beau's arms or the gentle sway of the boat in the bayou. I swung my legs over the side of the chaise, planting my feet on the cool floor as I tried to process everything that had just happened.

Beau had felt so real, so alive. The connection we shared was undeniable, transcending the physical and touching something deeper within me. Yet, as I sat there, the reality that I would probably never see him again weighed heavily on me. It was a strange sort of heartbreak, knowing that what we'd shared would remain in that fantasy space, locked away in a memory I would carry with me but never relive.

And yet, with the sadness came a quiet resolve. My time in Coral Cove wasn't over. Beau had taught me so much in those fleeting moments—how to slow down, how to find joy in the simple things, how to live in the present rather than constantly chasing the future. I owed it to myself to take those lessons to heart, to spend the rest of my time here embracing the peace and beauty that this seaside town had to offer.

I stood up, smoothing the wrinkles in my shirt,

my thoughts still swirling as I made my way to the curtain. Pushing it aside, I found Ms. Vesper waiting for me, her knowing eyes watching me with the same gentle warmth she had shown before.

"How do you feel?" she asked, her voice a soothing balm to my frayed emotions.

I took a deep breath, letting the air fill my lungs before releasing it slowly. "Different," I admitted, offering a small smile. "Better. But… there's a sadness too."

Ms. Vesper nodded, her expression wise and understanding. "That's natural, hon. Experiences like these can be powerful, even life-changing. They're meant to show you something, to teach you what you need to know. Sometimes, the hardest part is letting go."

I looked down, my thoughts still tangled with the emotions. "I'm not sure I'll ever let go of what I felt in there. But I know now that I needed it."

She stepped closer, placing her hand on my arm with a comforting touch. "That's the right attitude." She winked.

I nodded, feeling both gratitude and sadness swirling in my chest. "Thank you, for everything."

"You're welcome," she said, her smile warm

and reassuring. "Is there anything else I can do for you?"

I hesitated for a moment, then reached into my pocket for my wallet. "How much do I owe you for all of this?"

She waved her hand dismissively, her smile widening. "First experience is always free. But if you feel inclined, gratuities are always appreciated."

Without a second thought, I reached into my wallet and pulled out a crisp stack of bills—one thousand dollars. I placed it in her hand, watching as her eyes widened slightly before she looked back up at me with surprise and gratitude.

"This is for everything you've done," I said, my voice steady. "It was worth every penny."

Ms. Vesper's smile softened, a look of deep appreciation in her eyes as she accepted the money. "You're too kind. Thank you."

She tucked the money away and then, with a curious glint in her eye, she asked, "So how did it go? Was it everything you wanted?"

I paused, letting the memories of Beau flood back—his laughter, his love, the lessons he'd imparted, all rushing over me in a wave of warmth and nostalgia. A smile spread across my face as I remembered Beau's playful spirit, the way he made me feel alive and whole in a way I hadn't felt in years.

"Shabbow," I replied, the word rolling off my tongue with deep affection and satisfaction. "Shabbow."

THANKS FOR READING Seven of Pentacles. If you enjoyed it, please check out Harvesting Love, Steamy MM, Small Town, Second Chance, Thanksgiving Holiday Romance

Falling in love this Thanksgiving season. Park:

Being best friends with the boss has its perks.

Like a discount on the latest spicy MM romance.

Or the ability to knock off a bit early when a smokin' hot bibliophile pops into the shop.

The day before Thanksgiving, I had a chance encounter with a man that left us both feeling an undeniable chemistry between us.

Instead of the comforting scent of pumpkin pie, this holiday is filled with family anxiety.

Can I convince him to spend a little more time together, even if it's with my crazy family?

Falling in love this Thanksgiving season.

In the charming town of Coral Cove, Park is preparing for another Thanksgiving spent with family—while longing for someone to share his life with. Despite being surrounded by love, Park feels the weight of his loneliness as the holiday season approaches. When a handsome stranger walks into his small bookstore, Park's hope for a holiday romance sparks.

Ben Dawson is trying to escape the pain of losing his fiancé. A year after the tragic accident, he heads to Coral Cove on what was supposed to be their dream vacation. He's not expecting to find anything but bittersweet memories—until he meets Park, the adorable bookstore owner who makes Ben wonder if second chances at love are possible.

As Thanksgiving approaches, Park and Ben's chemistry ignites, leading them both to question their pasts, futures, and the magic of love that just might be waiting for them in the most unexpected of places.

Harvesting Love is a heartwarming and steamy MM romance set against the backdrop of the Thanksgiving season. Perfect for fans of small-town charm, second-chance love, and holiday magic, this book will capture your heart.

Sign up for Jax Wilder's newsletter and receive a collection of unpublished Coral Cove short stories. Meet familiar characters and dive deeper into the love and romance that Coral Cove is known for. Don't miss out on this exclusive content!

Jax Wilder

ALICE AND HER MAD HATTERS

A BISEXUAL REVERSE HAREM ROMANCE, ALICE IN WONDERLAND, PORTAL FANTASY ROMANCE

Jax Wilder

the FAE RINGS series

ALICE

AND HER

Mad Hatters

Bisexual Reverse Harem Romance

1

Coral Cove always felt a little... off. The kind of off that made people stop mid-step to catch their breath. he way the air hummed with a magic no one could ever quite name, how the sea breeze carried more than just salt and water but a whisper of something deeper. I felt it every time I wandered past the old shops, the odd charm of the place pulling at me, but nowhere as strongly as at *Lilly Drake*.

The chime of bells overhead greeted me as I stepped inside the shop, and immediately, I felt the familiar shift. It wasn't just a jewelry store—it was an escape. A place where the world outside didn't matter.

Lilly Drake wasn't like other jewelry shops. There

were no harsh displays of diamond rings or polished gold necklaces. Instead, fairy houses perched in the branches of miniature trees, delicate bridges connecting one whimsical nook to the next. Glass figures hung from the branches, catching the sunlight that filtered in through stained-glass windows, throwing rainbows across the room. The jewelry cases themselves were carved into the "forest," artfully nestled between moss-covered stones and twinkling crystals.

No, this wasn't an ordinary jewelry shop. It was something more, something alive.

"Ah, Alice. I knew you'd come in today." Rainbow Rivers' voice was soft and musical, like wind chimes on a spring afternoon. I turned to see Rainbow Rivers, gliding toward me like she was made of air. Her lavender hair caught the light, her eyes twinkling in a way that told me she knew things I didn't. Her eyes shimmered with a knowing smile, the kind that suggested she understood more than she ever let on.

I smiled, half-shrugging as I looked around. "I don't know why I love this place so much. It's... different. Magical. It just... calls to me."

Rainbow chuckled, her one of a kind hand made sparkling fairy wings fluttering ever so slightly.

"That's because *Lilly Drake* holds pieces of magic. Not everyone can see it, but you—" She looked me up and down, as if assessing my very soul. "You always feel it."

My hand drifted over one of the small branches, brushing my fingers across a necklace made of silver and opal stones. "I wouldn't say magic exactly," I replied, though I couldn't quite explain what it was either. "But it's like stepping into another world every time I walk through that door."

Rainbow arched an eyebrow. "And that's why you're here, isn't it?" she asked, that knowing smile still playing on her lips. "You want to escape."

I paused, my fingers tracing the cool surface of a silver pendent. I couldn't lie to her. "Yeah. Lately, it's all I want. I've been feeling... trapped. Like I'm just waiting for something to sweep me away, to take me out of this ordinary life and into something... more."

Rainbow hummed, disappearing behind one of the large trees. "So, you're looking for a little fantasy?"

"Exactly. I mean, who doesn't want to get lost in a good fantasy? Sometimes all I want is to curl up with one of those spicy novels from *Spellbound Stories* and just... disappear into the pages."

Rainbow reappeared, holding a small wooden box in her hands, her expression suddenly more serious. "What if I told you there was a way to disappear into something better than a book?"

I blinked, curiosity tugging at me. "What are you talking about?"

Without a word, she opened the box. Inside was a ring—a simple band of silver with a stone that shimmered like the sky at twilight, casting a thousand tiny rainbows across the shop.

The moment I saw it, I felt it. A hum in the air, like the ring was alive and waiting for me.

"It's beautiful," I breathed, my fingers itching to reach for it. "Can I try it on?"

Rainbow's lips curved into a sly smile, but she shook her head. "No. Not yet."

I frowned, confused. "What if it doesn't fit?"

"It will," she said, her voice confident. "They always do."

Something about the way she said it, like she knew a secret I didn't, made me pause. But I couldn't shake the pull of that ring, the way it seemed to call to me. I swallowed hard. "Okay. I'll take it."

Rainbow's expression softened, but there was a seriousness in her eyes now. She closed the box and held it out to me, her hand lingering on mine just a moment too long. "Before you go... a word of caution. Don't wear it unless you're absolutely sure. The ring knows where you belong. But if they aren't ready to let you come back..."

My heart skipped a beat. "They?"

Her eyes sparkled with something mischievous, something dangerous. "You'll see." She winked and turned away before I could press her for more.

I stood there for a moment, gripping the box in my hand, feeling the weight of her words settling over me like a thick fog. I had no idea what she meant by *they*, but something told me I wasn't going to get an answer.

With a soft thank you, I left *Lilly Drake* and stepped back into the sunlit streets of Coral Cove. The air felt warmer, thicker somehow, as I made my way to the park. The ring still sat in its little box, nestled safely in my bag, but I could feel it, like it was tugging at me, urging me to open it.

I reached the park and slowed my steps. The familiar sight of the swings greeted me, and I couldn't resist. I sat down on one of the old wooden seats, the chains creaking softly as I swung gently back and forth. My fingers found the box in my bag, pulling it out and holding it in my lap.

Rainbow's warning echoed. *Don't wear it unless you're sure.*

I opened the box, staring down at the ring. It glimmered in the fading sunlight, casting tiny rainbows across my skin. My heart thudded in my chest as I reached for it, my fingers trembling slightly.

What's the harm in trying it on?

With one last glance around the empty park, I slipped the ring onto my finger.

The world... shifted.

Everything around me shimmered, the colors vibrating, twisting. My breath caught in my throat as the park dissolved, the swing beneath me vanishing like smoke in the air.

I blinked, my heart racing as the world came back into focus.

I wasn't in the park anymore.

I was somewhere else. Somewhere... impossible.

2

I blinked, trying to shake off the haze that clung to me like fog. One second, I'd been sitting on a swing in Coral Cove, and now... what the hell?

The walls around me were mustard yellow and teal, corridors stretching in every direction like some kind of twisted maze. Everything looked like it had been decorated by someone with a grudge against color coordination. I turned in a slow circle, trying to make sense of this strange, claustrophobic place.

Where was I?

I took a few steps down one of the hallways, the silence so thick it felt like I was wrapped in it. "Hello?" My voice echoed back at me, bouncing off the walls.

No answer.

Great. This was just great. I had no idea where I was, no idea how I'd gotten here, and to top it all off, I was pretty sure I'd just seen a rabbit. A white rabbit.

It darted down a hallway to my left, disappearing around a corner. "Oh no, you don't." I muttered under my breath, more out of sheer stubbornness than anything else. If I was stuck in this place, I wasn't going to do it alone. Rabbit or not.

I hurried after it, turning the corner into another long corridor lined with doors. Each one was different—some big, some small, some carved with intricate designs. I stopped in front of a glass table in the middle of the hallway, the only thing that seemed remotely normal.

Sitting on the table was a small key and—was that a bottle? I picked up the key, examining it. It was tiny, barely bigger than my pinkie, and shaped like something from an old-timey fairytale. But it didn't fit any of the doors I'd tried so far.

I glanced at the bottle next. It was small, purple, and a little smoky, like one of those potions you'd see in a witch's shop. Of course, it had a label.

Drink Me.

I rolled my eyes. "Oh, of course. Because that's not suspicious at all."

I paused, feeling the dryness in my throat. I was thirsty. And assuming I wasn't tripping on something, what was the worst that could happen? Maybe this was all a dream, and I'd wake up soon, safe and sound in Coral Cove.

"Alright, Alice. What's the worst that could happen?" I muttered, popping the cork off the bottle. It smelled oddly sweet, like berries and something floral. Without thinking too much about it, I tipped the bottle back and took a gulp.

For a second, nothing happened.

Then, the world around me started to shift. I stumbled, grabbing the edge of the table as my body… shrank.

"What the—?" I gasped as the table grew taller, the floor rushing up to meet me. The hallways loomed above like a skyscraper, everything growing impossibly big, or maybe it was just me getting impossibly small. My heart pounded as I watched my hands shrink, the key in my palm suddenly feeling like a sword.

I blinked, trying to make sense of the rapid change. "This is… not ideal."

When the shrinking finally stopped, I was standing in a pile of fabric—my clothes. Of course, they hadn't shrunk with me. I looked down at myself, completely naked sans the ring on my finger and now smaller than a Barbie doll.

"Fantastic," I muttered, shaking my head. "At least I'm not cold."

My eyes fell on the key still clutched in my hand. It was big, almost as tall as I was now. An idea sparked, and I grabbed the edge of my discarded shirt, using the sharp corner of the key to slice through the fabric. In a matter of minutes, I had a makeshift dress—if you could call it that. It wasn't pretty, but it did the job.

I looked down at my handiwork and gave a half-hearted shrug. "Could be worse."

Once I'd dressed myself, I took stock of my surroundings again. The doors were even taller now, towering above me like the gates of some ancient fortress. My eyes scanned the room, and I spotted one door I hadn't noticed before. Smaller than the rest, tucked away in the corner.

I glanced at the key in my hand and then at the door.

"Worth a shot," I muttered, trudging over to the door and slipping the key into the lock.

It turned easily, the door swinging open with a soft creak. I stepped through, expecting another hallway or maybe a room. But no. I stepped out into… something else entirely.

The sky was pink. *Pink*. And the grass—well, it wasn't exactly grass. It shimmered, like a rainbow made out of thousands of tiny crystals, each one catching the light and sparkling in ways that couldn't be real.

"What the actual hell is this?" I whispered, taking a few hesitant steps forward. The trees around me were tall, their branches heavy with strange, oddly shaped fruits. Some of them looked like they belonged on Earth. Others… not so much.

I stared up at the sky, the impossible colors swirling above me like a kaleidoscope, and I couldn't help but laugh. "Someone definitely slipped me acid," I muttered. That was the only explanation, right? Some kind of weird trip. A dream. Anything but real life.

I sighed, shaking my head. "Okay, Alice. Time to figure out where the hell you are. And more importantly, how the hell to get out."

But as I stared at the shimmering landscape in front of me, a small voice in the back of my head whispered that maybe—just maybe—I wasn't going to wake up from this one.

3

I ambled along the vibrant path, absorbing the lush, unnatural beauty around me, when that familiar white blur—the rabbit—appeared again. It darted off the path, beckoning me into unknown territories. I knew better, I really did. But the curiosity that had led me to this bizarre world wasn't about to let a little wisdom get in the way now.

As I followed the white rabbit, weaving through an array of bizarrely colored trees, my foot caught on a hidden root. The world tilted dangerously. Panic clawed at my chest as the ground seemed to fall away beneath me. My arms flailed, grabbing at the air, as I pitched forward down a steep embankment. The descent was a chaotic blur of scratching branches and sharp stones that sent adrenaline surging through my veins like wildfire.

I crashed into the river with a shock that drove the breath from my lungs. The cold embrace of the water was a brutal awakening, grappling with the air in my lungs as I kicked desperately for the surface. Murky water blurred my vision, the current tugging at me, threatening to pull me back under. When my head finally broke free, I gasped, dragging the damp, heavy air into my chest.

Drenched and disoriented, I swam to the riverbank and clambered out. My heart pounded against my ribs, adrenaline still coursing through me as I stood there, water streaming from my clothes, pooling at my feet. The one thing I loathe—wet clothes clinging coldly to my skin.

With a huff, I trekked back to the path I'd strayed from, irritation prickling at every soaked step. "Great, just my luck to end up soaking wet in a land that probably doesn't even have towels," I muttered to myself. Then, a rueful smile tugged at my lips, "Or me someone who'd appreciate my dirty sense of humor."

Seeing no one around in this bizarre slice of the world, I decided to make the best of the sun's warmth. I stripped off my makeshift dress, draping it over a branch. There I was, standing naked under a foreign sky. It felt... exhilarating. Liberating and oddly arousing to be so vulnerable yet so unseen. I laid down on a patch of grass that sparkled under the sun, letting the strange, ticklish blades caress my bare skin.

"Anyone there?" I called out, half-expecting an answer. Silence greeted me, and I smiled, leaning back. My fingers began tracing idle, wandering paths across my skin, from my neck down to the curves of my breasts. The sensation was intoxicating—a blend of danger and desire, making my breath hitch.

I couldn't deny the heat building within me, an insistent pulse that demanded attention. My hand slipped lower, fingers exploring, stirring the warmth between my thighs into a fiery need. My touch was both question and answer, and as I found my slick, eager center, a low moan slipped from my lips.

"Fuck, that's good," I murmured to myself, my words a husky whisper against the backdrop of this strange, silent world. Alone, unseen, I let my inhibitions melt away like mist under the morning sun.

My gaze, heavy with desire, caught on a long, purple fruit dangling enticingly from a nearby tree. Its shape, unabashedly phallic, called to something primal within me. "Might as well see what all the fuss is about," I thought aloud, the words tinged with a playful curiosity as I reached for the fruit. It was firm, yet yielding, its surface ridged in a way that promised new depths of pleasure.

Clutching the fruit, I settled back into the grass, spreading my thighs wide to welcome this new companion. The initial touch of the cool fruit against my hot, flushed skin sent a shiver through me. "Oh, fuck yes," I exhaled as I guided it towards my dripping entrance. The cold was a sharp contrast, but as I slid the fruit inside, a delicious warmth began to spread through me, filling me, pushing me toward a precipice I hadn't known I was standing on.

I moved it slowly at first, savoring the sensation of being filled so completely. "Deeper," I gasped, urging myself on, my movements growing more urgent, more desperate. My free hand darted down to my clit, fingers circling with a fervor that matched the rhythmic thrusting of the fruit. "Yes, just like that," I moaned, the words spilling out in a breathy litany as I built myself toward climax.

My body tensed, the sensation coiling tightly within me, ready to snap. "I'm gonna come," I whispered fiercely, a declaration to the empty air.

The pleasure mounted, overwhelming, consuming, until it broke over me in a wild, explosive release that left me gasping, undone by my own hands, under the watchful eye of this alien sky.

As I lay there, breathless and basking in the afterglow, the reality of my solitude melded with the intensity of my release, leaving me with a sense of daring fulfillment that was as intoxicating as it was liberating.

It was only as I lay there, catching my breath, that I noticed—I wasn't alone. My eyes snapped open to find myself under scrutiny, the intensity of the gaze unmistakable even from a distance.

4

I stood abruptly, my heart racing as I realized I was no longer alone. Clumsily, I stumbled over myself, my cheeks flushing with heat as I reached for my now-dry dress strewn across the nearby branch. Pulling it on quickly, I turned to face the intruder.

There he was, a vision of absurdity and allure. His hot pink suit was a size too small, straining against muscles that seemed carved from marble, while his mustard yellow pants were an audacious choice that somehow worked. He wore a patchwork top hat, tilted jauntily over dark, tousled hair. His caramel skin and green eyes framed by a spray of freckles across his nose made him look like an artwork come to life.

I ran my fingers through my hair, trying to appear somewhat presentable despite the circumstances. This man had witnessed me fuck my pussy, and yet, there was no judgment in his eyes, only an intense curiosity that seemed to strip me bare once again.

He sauntered closer, each step a testament to his confident, almost predatory grace. With a flourish, he tipped his hat and bowed deeply. "Good day," he intoned with a smirk.

"Hello," I managed, voice wavering as I dipped into an awkward curtsy. "I was just, um…" My words trailed off, a pathetic attempt to explain my earlier indiscretion.

"No need for excuses here," he interrupted, his voice as smooth as velvet. "We're all mad in our own ways."

He ran his tongue along his lips, it was predatory and utterly mesmerizing. "My name is Hector Maddox, but my friends call me Hat."

"Alice," I replied, feeling the weight of his gaze like a physical touch.

"Alice," he repeated, savoring each syllable as if tasting a fine wine. "Such a lovely name for a lovely girl."

I felt a flush creep up my neck. "Were you

headed somewhere?" I asked, eager to change the subject.

"Indeed, I was on my way to a tea party," he said, eyes twinkling with mischief. "You must join me. It's not every day we get to feast with such... enticing company."

His words excited me, his gaze heavy with unspoken promises. I realized then just how hungry I was—not just for food but for the adventure he offered.

He seemed to read my thoughts, a sly smile playing on his lips. "Come, let's indulge in the madness together."

Without waiting for a formal agreement, he offered his arm, which I took, my body tingling with anticipation. As we began to walk, he did something wholly unexpected—instead of a dignified stroll, he began to skip, pulling me along in a whimsical dance down the path.

"Life is far too important to be taken seriously," he quipped as we skipped, his laughter like music.

As we moved through this lush, outlandish version of Wonderland, every sense was heightened. The colors seemed brighter, the sounds more melodious, and on the air was the delicate scent of blooming flowers and something more intoxicating —desire.

"So, Alice," Hat began, his voice low and inviting, "tell me something true about yourself."

"I'm usually not one for outdoor escapades," I confessed, feeling daring under his gaze.

"Ah, but today seems to be a day for shattering norms," he countered, his eyes gleaming with challenge.

As we approached the venue of the tea party, the whimsy of this wonderland unfurled before us in a breathtaking spectacle. The table, a long stretch of solid dark wood, was resplendent with flowers painted in a riot of colors that seemed to dance in the dappled sunlight. It rested under an avenue of trees from which odd trinkets and fruits dangled, swaying gently in the breeze.

Upon closer inspection, I noticed among the trinkets were fruits of the same purple variety I had encountered earlier. My cheeks flushed at the memory. Not far from them hung a cluster of pink fruits, their elongated, beaded structure reminiscent of anal beads, sparking a flutter of curiosity within me.

As I took my seat, it became apparent that the

guests at this gathering were all men, each adorned in elaborately colorful suits that defied the drab conventions of the ordinary world. Their attire shimmered with sequins and silks, making them look like princes from a particularly decadent court.

The first to introduce himself was a man in a peacock-blue suit with emerald green accents that matched his eyes. "I'm Jasper," he said, his voice smooth and enticing. "And I do hope you find the party... stimulating." His suggestive wink made me think of tangled sheets and whispered secrets.

Next to him sat a man, clad in a suit of deep violet with gold pinstripes. His dark hair was slicked back, and his eyes, a piercing slate gray, seemed to strip me down to my barest desires. "Elliot. Charmed, I'm sure," he murmured, his gaze lingering on me in a way that suggested he was imagining much more than just polite conversation.

On his other side was a man who introduced himself as Lucas. His suit was a brilliant shade of sunburst orange. His tousled blonde hair and easy smile gave him an approachable air, but the mischievous glint in his eye promised devilish fun. "Alice, lovely to meet a girl who knows how to enjoy the fruits of Wonderland," he joked, gesturing subtly to the hanging fruits with a playful raise of his eyebrows.

Completing the quartet was Nathaniel, wearing a suit of rich crimson that set off his dark skin and jet-black hair. His smile was slow and knowing, the kind that suggested he was well-versed in the art of pleasure. "Welcome to our little escape from reality," he said with a voice that caressed all the right nerves.

As we settled in, I found my gaze roaming from one man to the next, each more intriguing and attractive than the last. The air was intoxicating—lusty. The table was laden with an array of dishes that were as colorful and exotic as the men themselves, each plate promising a sensory overload.

Hat leaned closer, his breath tickling my ear. "Prepare yourself, Alice. This tea party is like none you've ever attended. Here, we feast on more than just food." His words, laced with a husky undertone, sent shivers down my spine.

The realization dawned on me: this wasn't just a feast for the stomach but for the senses, a playground of desires laid bare under the guise of a tea party. Each man seemed to offer a different temptation, a promise of pleasures untold.

As we took our seats among the madcap revelers, anticipation vibrated in the air. Promises were whispered in glances that undressed any façade I still had up. I knew one thing for certain: I was exactly where I needed to be, on the brink of indulging in the most decadent of delights.

5

As the tea party continued, the men around me whispered to each other, their voices a low hum beneath the clinking of teacups and laughter. My plate was an artist's palette of whimsical treats: mini sandwiches in funny shapes, brightly colored cookies, and cupcakes that looked too pretty to eat. Four cups of tea sat before me, each one a different shade of absurdity. Choosing the hot pink teacup with bright yellow flowers painted on it, I couldn't help but giggle at the sheer extravagance of it all.

Jasper, noticing my amusement, rose from his high-backed wooden chair and approached with a confidence that made my heart skip. "Would you like to take a stroll through the garden, Alice?" he asked, his voice a smooth invitation into the unknown.

"Carpe diem," I replied, embracing the spirit of adventure. He offered his hand with a gallant bend, and as I placed mine in his, he spun me behind his back and scooped me up onto his shoulders. His touch was a surprise, goosing my bum playfully, sending a delightful shiver through me. His strength was palpable; I felt weightless against his muscular frame. As he hopped forward, each bounce sent thrilling vibrations to my center, the friction stirring a delicious warmth within me.

The garden that unfolded before us was a vivid tapestry of colors, predominantly red with roses so deeply hued they seemed almost unreal. "It's beautiful," I breathed, lost in the enchantment of the place.

Jasper set me down gently among the flowers, his hands lingering just a moment too long on my hips. "We're in a little subsection of the Fae realm called Wonderland," he explained, his voice lowering as he guided me through the blooms. "And it's all ruled by the Red Queen. She's... formidable, to say the least, and not one to be crossed."

The way he spoke of the queen sent a chill

down my spine. "What happens if you break her rules?" I asked, my voice barely above a whisper.

"Death," he replied somberly. "She does not take kindly to disobedience."

Despite the warning, the danger seemed distant, almost like part of a game—one I was more than willing to play. Jasper's closeness was intoxicating, his every touch sending chills down my spine. He played with a strand of my hair, his fingers skilled and teasing. "What's your favorite flower?" he asked suddenly.

I glanced around at the vibrant display surrounding us. "I've always been a fan of lavender," I confessed, the scent already mingling in the air, subtle yet pervasive.

Jasper smiled, his eyes glinting with mischief. "A choice as enchanting as you are, Alice." He gestured expansively to the garden around us. "Here, the Red Queen prefers the red roses—she believes they symbolize the strength and blood of her reign. Picking one without permission is said to bring... certain doom."

His words hung between us, laden with an unspoken warning. Yet, as my eyes caught the brilliant red of the roses, curiosity overcame caution. I reached out and plucked a single rose, its petals as soft as velvet against my fingers. Jasper watched me, a curious expression on his face, but he said nothing about my bold move.

"The Red Queen sounds terrifying," I murmured, twirling the rose by its stem.

"She can be, but Wonderland is full of secrets and delights that often outweigh the dangers," Jasper replied, drawing closer. His hand brushed mine, sending a jolt of electricity through me. "Would you like to explore some of those delights with me?" His voice was a velvet caress, promising pleasures untold.

"When in Rome—or Wonderland," I laughed softly, the thrill of the unknown coursing through me. "Lead the way."

Jasper offered a roguish grin and led me deeper into the garden. "Wonderland has a way of amplifying everything—feelings, sensations... desires." He plucked a sprig of lavender and handed it to me. "Smell this, and tell me if it doesn't make the world seem brighter."

I inhaled deeply, the familiar, soothing scent of lavender filling my senses, making the colors of the garden seem even more vivid. "It's wonderful," I sighed, a smile spreading across my face.

"And it's just the beginning," Jasper murmured.

His fingers traced a line down my arm, raising goosebumps. "Imagine what other sensations await."

Captivated by his words and the promise in his eyes, I nodded, eager to experience everything he was offering. As he leaned in, his breath warm against my cheek, he whispered, "Let's find a more secluded spot, where I can show you just how pleasurable Wonderland can be."

I looked him up and down, taking in the strength in his frame and the mischievous spark in his eyes. "Yes, a thousand percent yes," I said.

With that, Jasper took my hand, leading me through the maze of flowers and scents, towards a hidden alcove draped in wisteria. The world seemed to fall away, leaving only the promise of ecstasy, the danger of the queen's rules a distant thought against the backdrop of impending delight.

He handed me the flowers, and as I inhaled deeply, the world around us seemed to shimmer even brighter. Jasper traced a finger down my arm, raising goosebumps on my skin. "Come to me, Alice," he beckoned, leading me deeper into the garden.

I followed, plucking a red rose along the way, and soon found myself in a field of lavender under a pink, swirling sky. Laying back among the fragrant blooms, Jasper produced a peacock feather as if from thin air and began to trace it along my arms, neck, and back.

"Your beauty is unparalleled, Alice," he whispered, his voice heavy with desire. "Every curve, every breath... I want to explore all of you."

Encouraged by his words, I let my makeshift dress fall away, feeling bold and utterly captivated. He watched me with intense appreciation, a deep chuckle escaping him. "Do you want to wear my hat?" he teased, offering it to me with a playful grin.

Slipping the hat on, it fell over my eyes, and I giggled, feeling like a character in our own private play. "Is it okay if I kiss you?" he murmured, his breath hot against my skin.

"Yes," I breathed out eagerly, pulling the hat up to meet his lips.

"But I didn't want to kiss you there," he teased, his lips wandering to my neck, then lower, each kiss igniting a fire within me. He worshipped my body with his mouth, exploring each part of me with a reverent intensity. When he reached my hips, he paused, his breath warm against my mound.

Spreading my legs, I invited him closer, and he didn't hesitate. His tongue found my heat, teasing at my slit before focusing on my clit. The sensation was overwhelming, a crescendo of pleasure that built with every flick and suck.

"I need more," I gasped, lost in the sensation and desperate for him to fill me.

Jasper looked up, his eyes dark with desire that seemed to capture the very essence of twilight. "I thought you'd never ask," he murmured, his voice a low rumble that vibrated through my very core. He positioned himself between my thighs, his presence electrifying. As he entered me, the world seemed to shift into a spectrum of pulsing colors. The sky above us blazed with hues of pink and violet, each shade shimmering in time with our rhythm. It was an orchestra of light and sensation, unlike anything I had ever experienced.

Every touch was intensified by the magic of this place, every movement resonated through my body like a chord struck on a celestial harp. Jasper moved with a purposeful grace, exploring every contour of my being, his hands tracing the arcs and valleys of my form as if he were learning a sacred text.

As he drove deeper, a coiling tension wound its way through my limbs, anchoring me to the spot, yet urging me to soar. I felt it in my clenched toes, in my arched back, in the breath that I held tight within my lungs. The world narrowed to the point of exquisite pressure where our bodies joined, each thrust pushing me closer to the edge of an abyss I yearned to tumble into.

He whispered promises, each one a vow to take me higher, to push me further into the realm of ecstasy. "I'm going to make you come," he assured, his voice thick with the power of impending fulfillment. His words were both a command and an invocation, summoning a climax that built like a storm on the horizon.

The sky seemed to shutter with color, a kaleidoscope that mirrored the crescendo of sensations that overwhelmed me. It was incredible, a symphony of light and touch that stole the very breath from my lungs. I had never done drugs, but I imagined no high could possibly compare to the intensity of this moment. The world spun, the colors danced, and I was adrift in a sea of pleasure so profound it seemed to transcend the boundaries of reality.

With a final, deep thrust, he sent me spiraling over the edge. My climax washed over me in waves, each one a crashing surge that left me shuddering and gasping. Jasper held me close as I trembled, his arms a fortress against the quaking of my limbs, his breath a warm caress against the shell of my ear.

"We're here together, in this wonder," he whispered, his lips brushing against my skin, imprinting his words like a seal upon my heart.

As we lay there, wrapped in each other's arms among the fragrant lavender and roses, the garden around us seemed to settle, as if it too had been caught up in our storm. A profound peace enveloped us, and in that serene aftermath, I knew that Wonderland had claimed not just a piece of my heart, but whispered promises of belonging that I was only just beginning to understand.

The return to the tea party found me feeling ravenous, as though my earlier exploits with Jasper had awakened not just new desires but a profound hunger as well. I glanced at the ornate clock perched near the spread of treats—it stubbornly marked six o'clock, just as it had when I first arrived.

"Is it still tea time?" I asked, a hint of amusement coloring my tone.

"It's always six o'clock here. Not time for anything else but tea, and enjoying the company of those around us," Hat quipped, his smile infectious.

Laughing, I decided to simply surrender to the whimsy of this place. I indulged in the spread before me: sandwiches layered with exotic, vibrant fillings that melted on the tongue, cookies dotted with unknown but delicious bits, and a peculiar gelatin dessert that shimmered under the light. Each bite was a discovery, a celebration of flavors so decadent that they seemed to dance on my palate. I sipped on a tea that was a curious blend of sweet and spicy, its steam carrying tales of distant, spicy shores.

After gloriously gorging, I patted my stomach, slightly overwhelmed by the feast. "I need to walk off this full tummy," I stood with a slight groan of contentment.

Elliot, who had been quietly observing from the edge of the gathering, rose smoothly to his feet. "May I suggest a stroll by the lake? It's quite a sight under the moonlight," he offered, his voice carrying the soft promise.

Intrigued, I nodded.

Elliot led me down a winding path that seemed to be lit by the natural luminescence of the night itself. As we approached the lake, the sight took my breath away. Not one, but three moons hung in the sky, each casting a different gentle light onto the landscape: one silver, another pale blue, and the third a soft, ghostly green. The reflections danced across the water's surface in a mesmerizing ballet of light.

"The moons of Wonderland," Elliot began, his voice smooth as velvet in the tranquil night, "are more than celestial bodies; they are the source of our realm's magic. Each moon influences different elements of our world and ourselves. They can amplify emotions, enhance sensations, and even manipulate time."

"They are said to reflect not just light, but the very essence of those who gaze upon them. What do you see in their reflection, Alice?"

I peered into the lake, watching the triple reflections ripple and transform with the gentle lapping of the water. "I see... possibility," I murmured, captivated by the shifting patterns.

Elliot nodded, a smile playing at the corners of his mouth. "Possibility is a powerful thing. It can shape empires, and it can define who we choose to be," he said, his gaze intense as it met mine. "In Wonderland, we are often who we believe ourselves to be, reflected back at us in myriad ways."

His words wove through the cool night air, crafting an atmosphere thick with introspection. "And who do you believe yourself to be, Alice, here in this place of eternal tea parties and moonlit lakes?"

I was silent for a moment, considering his question. It was one thing to play along with the madness of Wonderland, but another to confront what this world was mirroring about my innermost self. "I think... I'm someone who's looking for more than what I've known. Someone who's not afraid to explore who I might be."

"Exploration is an art," Elliot responded, his voice soft yet compelling. "And like all art, it requires both courage and vulnerability. Here by this lake, under the gaze of three moons, you can dare to explore, to see the parts of yourself that you hide from the world."

"Wonderland is a reflection, Alice. It shows us not just what we are, but what we can become." Elliot stepped closer, his presence enveloping. "What do you want to become?"

Captivated, I watched as the moonlight played on the lake, its surface shimmering with the magic that Elliot described. "How does the magic influence all this?" I gestured to the expanse of the lake and the vibrant flora surrounding us.

Elliot smiled, a knowing twinkle in his eye. "Watch." He guided me to a cluster of roses, bathed in the tri-moonlight, their red petals so deep they were nearly black. "These roses thrive under the moon's magic. Smell one, but remember—just smell, don't pluck. Their scent is intoxicating, enhanced by the moons to heighten all of your senses."

Tentatively, I leaned in and inhaled the fragrance of a rose. The effect was immediate and profound; my skin tingled as if the petals themselves were brushing against me, and every sound and color around me seemed amplified. The magic of the moons made the world around me vibrate with an intensity that was almost palpable.

Elliot's hand found the small of my back, sending a jolt of electricity through me. "Embrace what Wonderland has to offer," he murmured into my ear, his breath warm against my neck.

As he traced invisible lines down my arms, his touch sparked trails of goosebumps, heightening my already sensitized skin. He stepped closer, and I could feel the heat of his body even without direct contact. Encouraged by his closeness, I reached back, my hands finding the contours of his form through his clothes. My fingers brushed against the outline of his arousal, and I grasped him gently, confirming what my body already knew—he wanted me as much as I did him.

With a fluid motion, I let my makeshift dress fall to the ground, the fabric whispering against my skin as it pooled at my feet. I bent forward, the position exposing me to the cool night air and to Elliot's gaze. He caressed my buttocks, his hands strong yet gentle, before slipping a finger along my wetness. His touch was expert, knowing, sending waves of pleasure coursing through me as he found my most sensitive spots.

Elliot's voice was low, almost reverent as he whispered, "You're exquisite, Alice. Every inch of you responds so beautifully." He encouraged my hips back towards him, and I felt his hardness teasing at my entrance.

"I need to feel you inside of me," I breathed out, the desire clear in my voice.

"That's the roses talking," he teased, his breath hot against my ear.

"I was ready to fuck you the first time I laid eyes on you," I shot back, the boldness of the environment emboldening me further.

Without another word, he entered me, his thrusts deliberate and deep. Each movement was synchronized with the pulsating light of the moons, each stroke pushing us both toward a climax that seemed to be written in the stars above. As he brushed against my puckered hole with his thumb, I gasped, the sensation new and electrifying.

"More," I begged, and he obliged by slipping his thumb inside, slowly stretching me in ways that had my entire body trembling. The world around us seemed to explode in a crescendo of moonlit ecstasy as I came, waves of intense pleasure radiating from where we joined to every extremity.

Laying there by the reflective lake, under the watchful eyes of the three moons, wrapped in the arms of Elliot, I knew Wonderland wasn't just a place, but a state of being—transformative, magical, and utterly intoxicating.

7

"Time really is just a suggestion here, isn't it?" I asked, my tone laced with amusement as Hat topped off my tea with a flourish.

"It's always six o'clock," Lucas chimed in with a wink.

Feeling delightfully sated by the food and tea, I pushed back from the table with a groan of contentment.

Lucas rose, offering his hand with a gallant flair. "Allow me to guide you through our rose maze. It's not just a walk; it's an experience." His voice was a seductive whisper.

Intrigued by the anticipation in his eyes, I followed him into a labyrinth where the air was a perfume of roses and mystery. "Each turn holds a surprise," Lucas explained as we approached the first corner.

He paused and produced a pair of benwa balls from his pocket, their silver surface gleaming seductively. "These will enhance every step you take," he murmured, his voice low and enticing as he placed them in my hand. His fingers brushed against mine, sending a shivers up my arm.

With a mix of excitement and a flush of daring, I allowed him to guide me in inserting the benwa balls. The sensation was immediate—a delicious, subtle pressure that promised to build with each step. "You'll find they add quite the thrill to our little journey," he assured me, a wicked grin playing across his lips.

As we ventured deeper into the maze, the path turned and revealed a new surprise. Lucas stopped before a pair of delicate nipple clamps adorned with tiny roses. "These will sharpen your pleasure," he explained, his hands deftly applying the clamps. The slight pinch was a perfect echo to the internal sensations, and a dual wave of pleasure began to pulse through me.

Another turn brought us to a mysterious setup: a bar with cuffs. "For a touch of restraint," he whispered, his breath hot against my ear as he secured my ankles, spreading me open with an intimacy that drew a gasp from my lips.

The vulnerability was exhilarating, heightening the sensations that the maze conjured within me. I was open, exposed, and teetering on the edge of overwhelming pleasure. "Lucas, please," I found myself begging, a desperate need to climax building within me.

With a predatory smile, Lucas knelt before me. He lifted my cuffed legs slightly, his tongue finding my eager clit. The world narrowed to the point of his tongue and the relentless pressure of the benwa balls. His mouth was skilled, each flick and suckle pushing me closer to the brink.

"More, please," I gasped, lost in the sensation.

In a swift motion, Lucas stood, releasing his arousal. He entered me in one fluid thrust, filling me completely, intensifying the sensation of the benwa balls inside me. I dug my fingers into the earth as he moved, each thrust more insistent than the last. His rhythm was relentless, and when he brought me to climax, I screamed, a raw sound of intense release that echoed off the maze walls.

But one climax wasn't enough for Lucas. He kept moving, building me up swiftly again. As he thrust, he rubbed my clit, pushing me over into another explosive orgasm. His own climax followed, marked by a groan of release as he filled me with his warmth.

Afterwards, Lucas gently removed the benwa balls, the cuffs, and the nipple clamps, each movement tender and caring. He held me close, his voice soft and full of wonder. "You're incredible, Alice. Absolutely magical."

In Lucas's arms, amidst the tangled paths of the rose maze, I realized that Wonderland wasn't just a place of whimsy and madness—it was a realm where every hidden desire could come to life, where every fantasy was just around the corner, waiting to be discovered and explored.

8

Back at the tea table, the world of Wonderland sprawled around us like a canvas of absurd delights. Here, sex toys sprouted on trees as naturally as apples, and laughter seemed to bubble up from the very ground. The vibrant, surreal landscape was a playground for the senses, where happiness wasn't just around every corner—it practically paved the streets.

I indulged in more of the exotic, tantalizing, sometimes phallic food, each bite a burst of joy on my tongue. The tea party was in full swing, the air carried on it the rich aroma of spiced tea and the sound of carefree conversations.

"You know," I started, a mischievous glint in my

eye, "I wish Wonderland had a playground. Swinging sounds like such fun here."

Hat, always quick on the uptake, exchanged a knowing look with Nathaniel. "Oh, but we do have a playground," he said, his voice laced with double entendre. "Perhaps a little stroll to stretch our legs?"

Nathaniel's smile was slow and seductive. "Indeed, it's not far. A place to really swing to your heart's content," he added, the twinkle in his eyes unmistakable.

Intrigued and more than a little excited by the prospect, I agreed, and we set off down a path that seemed to beckon us forward with its clear, inviting trail. It led us to an adult playspace that redefined the concept of a playground. Traditional swings were replaced with luxurious sex swings, and there were artfully arranged stations for bondage, complete with silky ropes and elegant restraints.

The sight of the elaborate setups, designed for all manner of pleasurable pursuits, had my body tingling with anticipation. The thought of being with both Hat and Nathaniel in such an environment sent a rush of heat through me.

As we entered, the rules of this playspace were clear—consent was paramount, each action and gesture needing affirmation. Hat turned to me, his gaze intense. "Do you consent to exploring your boundaries with us, Alice?" he asked, his voice both commanding and caring.

With a nod, I gave my permission, excitement coursing through me at the prospect of such an adventure. Nathaniel stepped forward, his presence just as commanding. "And I submit to your desires as well, Alice. Guide us through your fantasies."

The dynamic of control shifted fluidly between us. Hat directed me with a firm yet respectful tone. "Undress, Alice," he instructed, watching intently as I complied. "Yes, sir," I responded, feeling a thrill at the command.

Soon, I was strapped into a sex swing, the cool air of Wonderland kissing my bare skin. Hat and Nathaniel adjusted the straps, ensuring I was comfortable yet completely exposed. Hat, noticing my flushed cheeks and quick breath, praised me, "You're such a good girl, Alice." I realized then how much his approval exhilarated me.

With my consent, Hat blindfolded me, plunging my world into darkness. The absence of sight heightened my other senses to an almost unbearable intensity. I felt a feather-like caress trail up my inner thighs, teasing over my skin and sending shivers through my body.

Then, without warning, a firmer touch snapped a whip against my buttocks. The sting was startling yet strangely delightful. As I rocked back and forth on the swing, the blend of pain and pleasure melded into a symphony of sensations.

A warm breath teased my ear before a tongue lavished attention on my throbbing clit. The rhythmic licking pushed me to the brink of ecstasy. "Please, more," I gasped, desperate for the fulfillment only a cock could provide.

uddenly, fulfilling my plea, someone—his identity obscured by the blindfold's darkness—thrust into me. His cock drove deep, each movement forceful yet calculated, as if he were both claiming and worshipping my body with each stroke. The intensity of his thrusts catapulted me over the edge into a staggering, all-consuming orgasm. My body arched instinctively, straining against the soft constraints of the swing, as wave after wave of pleasure crashed over me. My breath caught in bursts, my voice a crescendo of gasps and moans that filled the air.

As the waves of my climax ebbed into satisfying aftershocks, I reached up and yanked off the blindfold, the sudden return of light momentarily disorienting. My eyes focused, and there he was—Hat, his expression one of intense satisfaction mixed with tender care. His body still joined with mine, he smiled down at me, his cock still erect, pulsing gently inside me. With a grace that spoke of deep familiarity, he began to kiss his way up my body. Each kiss was a seal of the pleasure we shared, starting from my thighs and moving upwards, igniting tiny fires on my skin wherever his lips touched.

Breathless and still reeling from the heights we had reached, I turned my gaze towards Nathaniel, who had been watching us with a look of intense desire etched across his features. "Lick me clean," I commanded, my voice thick with the remnants of pleasure and the authority of newfound desires awakened in this Wonderland's embrace.

Nathaniel moved forward without hesitation, his movements eager and fluid. He knelt between my widely spread legs, his eyes locked on mine as he leaned in. His tongue, skilled and warm, met the sensitive flesh still pulsing from my recent climax. He licked delicately at first, savoring the mix of our mingled juices, before his actions became more purposeful—his tongue drawing broad, firm strokes designed to rekindle the fire that had barely begun to wane.

The sensation of being cleaned by such a devoted, attentive mouth was profoundly erotic, sending ripples of pleasure coursing through me once again. Nathaniel's dedication to the task, his eagerness to taste and please, drew me rapidly back to a peak of arousal. Just as I felt myself nearing the brink once more, he paused, his gaze intense and questioning, seeking permission for something more.

With a nod, I invited him to continue, and he shifted his position. Aligning himself with the entrance of my still-throbbing center, he entered me smoothly, his cock sliding in with an ease born of our combined slickness. Nathaniel filled me completely, his strokes deep and sure, pushing me further into a spiral of ecstasy. Each thrust was a perfect counterpoint to Hat's earlier fervor, and together, they played me like an instrument tuned to the key of pleasure.

Nathaniel's pace quickened, his movements becoming more urgent as he drove us both toward another explosive climax. The sensation of being so thoroughly possessed, so deeply cherished by these two men, was overwhelming. When the climax broke over me, it was with a force that blurred the edges of reality, the pleasure so intense that for a moment, I wondered if I had transcended into another realm entirely.

After the waves of ecstasy had finally subsided, leaving me languid and utterly spent, Nathaniel gently withdrew. Both he and Hat, with careful and tender motions, helped me out of the swing, their arms supporting me as my legs trembled with residual pleasure. Hat's embrace enveloped me, his strength a comforting presence as he carried me away from the playground, cradling me against his chest.

As we left the adult playspace behind, the echoes of our shared ecstasy lingered in the air, a sweet melody of fulfilled desires and explored boundaries that promised even more wonders in the days to come in Wonderland.

The roses had seemed harmless enough, and I'd indulged in picking them without a second thought. Their vibrant colors, the velvet-soft petals between my fingers—it had all felt like a simple pleasure, a small rebellion against the strangeness of Wonderland. But now, as I stand here and face the Queen's knight, the weight of my actions settles over me like a shroud.

The knight regards me with an impassive stare, his presence as imposing as the armored horses I'd seen galloping through Wonderland's gardens. "Alice, by order of the Queen of Hearts, you're to remain here until she arrives," he declares, his tone leaving no room for negotiation. "She'll be arriving promptly at six o'clock."

I glance at the clock tower, but it's always six here, always teatime. I swallow, a hint of unease curling through me as the knight lifts a trumpet to his lips, the piercing notes announcing the Queen's impending arrival. It dawns on me that, perhaps, I'd underestimated Wonderland's rules—and the consequences of breaking them.

The Queen of Hearts enters in a rush of color and presence, sweeping into the room with a fluid grace that borders on lethal. She's taller than I imagined, wearing a scarlet ballgown that plunges down to an innie belly button, long red hair cascading over bare shoulders. She is, without a doubt, the most stunning woman I have ever seen. There's a dark allure to her, a power that prickles across my skin and sends a shiver through me.

Around me, the Hatters drop to their knees, bowing their heads in reverence, and I realize with growing unease that I am the only one left standing. A guard to my left growls, "Kneel before your Queen!"

It takes a beat for me to understand they're talking to me, and I falter, pointing to myself as if to clarify. The Queen steps forward, her lips curling into a smirk as she regards me with an intensity that makes my stomach flip.

"Alice of Wonderland," she begins, only for me to interrupt her.

"I'm not from Wonderland," I say quickly, but my words barely matter.

The Queen tilts her head, amusement flickering in her eyes. "Alice in Wonderland, you plucked my roses, and now you refuse to kneel? You're a bold one." She raises a finger and brushes it along my cheek, then tilts my chin up, forcing me to meet her gaze. "I am your Queen."

The words come sharp, cutting through the air with an authority that makes me tingle. I open my mouth to protest, but she holds up a hand, stopping me.

"For this offense, I think a fitting punishment is in order. I believe three roses were plucked, yes? Three times, then, shall you be punished."

A rush of heat blooms in my cheeks, but I nod, letting my gaze fall. I'm mesmerized by the challenge in her eyes, by the sharpness of her presence. "I accept your punishment," I murmur, not entirely sure what to expect.

She steps closer, guiding me over to the table. I bend over at her silent command, my breath hitching as she lifts my skirt. The room feels charged, like we're at the edge of a thunderstorm.

Her breath is warm against my ear as she leans in, her voice low and sultry. "You've been a very bad girl, Alice. Plucking my roses, flouting my laws. You deserve to be taught a lesson."

"How bad was I?" I ask, surprised by the anticipation in my own voice.

"Oh, terrible," she purrs, running a hand along my backside. "You'll think twice before touching what's mine."

Her palm lands on my bare skin, a sharp, stinging slap that leaves me gasping. The pain blurs into pleasure, and I arch my back, pressing into her touch as she strokes the place she just struck. Her hand moves slowly, teasing over the curve of my hips, then down further, fingers trailing across my inner thighs and pressing into my slick heat. My body shudders as she runs her fingers along the length of me, finding me wet and wanting. She knows it, too, and I can feel her smile against my neck as she traces delicate circles over my clit, making me gasp.

My moans echo finding the ears of every onlooker, her fingers skillfully teasing my body, drawing me closer to the edge. Just as I think I might lose myself in the sensation, she pulls back, only to bring her palm down on me again, harder this time. I cry out, a mixture of shock and pleasure spilling from my lips.

The Queen doesn't pause. Her fingers slip back between my legs, pushing into me, filling me. I let out a strangled moan, my body curling into her touch, heat coiling deep in my belly as she moves, relentless and controlled. Her other hand presses down on my back, pinning me in place as she parts my legs and enters me further. Her fingers thrust deep, then slow, twisting inside me as she drives me closer to the brink.

My breath hitches, and I can feel myself beginning to unravel, but just before I reach the peak, she withdraws, leaving me empty and aching. Another slap lands on my backside, sharper this time, and I yelp, feeling the sting race up my spine.

"You've taken three roses," she murmurs, her voice like silk over gravel, "so I'll make sure you're thoroughly punished for each." She trails her hand over my thighs, her fingers finding my clit again, rubbing in circles that send shivers through me. Her other hand cups my breast, squeezing just enough to make me gasp. She leans in, her breath hot on my ear. "If you ever touch my roses again, I'll see to it that you never feel the hot rush of pleasure again."

I let out a strangled moan, hips bucking into her touch. The world fades away until it's just us, her fingers working me, her presence filling every corner of my senses. She's close, so close I can feel the warmth of her body against mine, and her scent surrounds me, intoxicating and heady.

When she pulls back, it's like being doused in ice water, but before I can protest, she lifts me upright and hands me a cool rag. I shake my head, declining it, not wanting to break the spell just yet.

"Good," she purrs, and then her lips are on mine, soft but insistent. I can taste her, feel her, every nerve alight as she pulls away, leaving me breathless, suspended on the edge of something I can't quite name.

10

The Queen of Hearts had swept away, her regal presence leaving the air thick with lingering tension. The Hatters, as if freed from an enchantment, picked up right where they'd left off, pouring tea into chipped cups and chattering as if nothing had happened. I watched them for a moment, their laughter strangely hollow in my ears, and felt an odd sense of disconnection. It was like I was slipping back into myself, as if I'd been pulled out of a trance.

I traced my fingers over the ring on my hand, the delicate band warm against my skin. A shiver of déjà vu rippled through me as I recognized the faint etching along its surface. Memories flooded back, bringing with them the scent of herbs and old wood, and Rainbow's voice from the jewelry store —Lilly Drake—floating in my mind like a forgotten warning.

The name came back to me: Lilly Drake. Rainbow had been so clear, hadn't she? She'd said something about the ring's power and the caution it required. I recalled her exact words now: "The rings don't always let you go back if they're not done with you." I gazed around at Wonderland, at the distorted landscape that had so thoroughly seduced me with its freedom, its danger, and its delicious, unpredictable rewards.

But then there was that choice, the one lingering in the back of my mind, heavier now with what I knew. I could return to my life in Coral Cove, where things were mundane and ordinary but also safe. Or I could stay here, forever dancing on the knife's edge between liberation and peril.

I took a deep breath, slipping the ring from my finger. The world seemed to fold in on itself, twisting into a kaleidoscope of color and light. I closed my eyes, feeling the air thicken around me, and when I opened them again, I was standing back in Coral Cove, the ocean breeze cool against my skin. It felt jarring and surreal, as though I'd fallen through a trapdoor from one world to the next. I looked down at myself and caught the scent clinging to my clothes—a mixture of sweat, roses, and sex. I needed a shower.

At home, I let the water wash over me, the warmth easing the tension in my muscles. I felt both drained and energized, an odd contradiction, as if my body had been through a war while my mind was still coming to terms with it all. It was hard to shake the feeling of hands on my skin, the echo of the Queen's touch, and that dark thrill of submitting to her power. The memory left me tingling even now, my body still singing from the experience.

By the time I tumbled into bed, I was half-asleep, Wonderland lingering like an imprint on my closed eyelids. I drifted off, uncertain of where I might wake up next.

When morning arrived, the first place I went was back to Lilly Drake. I stepped through the shop's familiar door, its little bell chiming above me, and there was Rainbow behind the counter, as if she'd been expecting me.

"I see you made it back," she said, a knowing smile on her lips.

"Was it real?" I asked, my voice softer than I'd intended. "It felt… I don't know. It felt too intense to be just a dream."

"Oh, it's real all right," she replied, leaning in. "The Fae realm doesn't play by our rules. The pleasures, the dangers—they're all real. When you put that ring on, you're entering their world, and once you're there, it's as much a part of you as you are of it. If you're not certain you want to be there, Alice, and the ring decides to keep you… that will be your reality."

I felt my heart skip, a cold shiver traveling up my spine as her words sank in. The idea that I could've stayed there, perhaps forever, seemed both exhilarating and terrifying.

"Here," I said, sliding the ring across the counter to Rainbow. "I don't think I'm ready to be tempted by it again. Not just yet."

Rainbow nodded, understanding etched into the lines around her eyes. "You're wiser than most. But if you ever change your mind, you know where to find me." She closed her hand over the ring, but I couldn't help but feel the way its absence left my hand oddly bare. I turned to leave, but not without one last glance at the small, unassuming piece of jewelry in her palm.

As I stepped back into the street, I found myself mulling over everything I'd experienced, the rush of Wonderland still thrumming beneath my skin. The choice to leave had been mine, but the taste of that other world lingered, and I knew that someday I might feel its pull again.

For now, though, I walked through Coral Cove with a new appreciation for the quietness, the ordinariness. I saw the world around me differently—its colors, its edges, and its hidden corners. I had glimpsed what was possible, both magical and mundane, and I knew I had the courage to explore either path.

The ring might have been out of sight, but its power, and the thrill of choosing my own fate, remained with me. For the first time, I felt ready to embrace the unknown, no matter which world it might lead me to next.

IF YOU LIKED Alice and Her Mad Hatters, then please check out my other series, Tarot Fantasies.

THE DEVIL'S Temptation
One card, one choice, ultimate temptation.

. . .

Dottie:

I never believed in fairy tales or silly things like romantic love.

But I drew The Devil card, and his name was Lucian.

When I laid eyes on him, I knew I wouldn't leave The Arcane Room as the same virgin who walked in.

Magic was only real in stories.

Or was it?

Sign up for my newsletter and get a free book today! https://mailchi.mp/158597581671/jax-wilder

Jax Wilder

ALSO BY JAX WILDER

CORAL COVE SERIES

Sleighed by Love

Harvesting Love

Dawning Desire

Knead You Now

Love Rewound

Perfect Lover Spell

Haunted by Her

Red, White, and Ravished

TAROT FANTASIES SERIES

The Devil's Temptations

Strength of the Beast

Hanged Passions

Six of Cups

Death's Embrace

Queen of Pentacles

Seven of Pentacles

Ace of Wands

Three of Swords

Lovers In The Veil

<u>Two of Swords</u>

Seven of Wands

The Star

Coastal Cupid Series

HeartBound Souls

Witches of Coral Cove

From Hell With Love

FAE RING SERIES

Alice and Her Mad Hatters

Bound By The Glass Slipper

STAND ALONE TITLES

Pride and Prejudice and Witches

ADDITIONAL BOOKS BY RAINBOW QUARTZ PUBLISHING

MIRANDA LEVI

From A Youth A Fountain Did Flow

The Sea Withdrew

A Tear In Time

Mother Nature

In Orion's Hands

JACKSON ANHALT

From The 911 Files

Isla Watts

A Fairy Bad Day

Surprise! You're a Vampire

Gorgeous, Gorgeous, Gorgons

Mork The Handsome Orc

Adopted By Werewolves

Bite Me If You Can

That's The Spirit!

Illiana Barret

Prompted: 2,339 Romance Prompts: A Writer's Essential Resource

Prompted 1,700 Fantasy Prompts: A Writer's Essential Resource

Prompted 1,605 Science Fiction Writing Prompts: A Writer's Essential Resource

Prompted 1,902 Horror Writing Prompts : A Writer's Essential Resource

Prompted 1,290 Mystery Writing Prompts : A Writer's Essential Resource

Prompted 1,582 Children's Book Writing Prompts: A Writer's Essential Resource

Prompted: 2,265 Historical Fiction Writing Prompts : A Writer's Essential Resource

Prompted 1,500 Steampunk Writing Prompts

Prompted: 1,600 Dystopian Prompts: A Writer's Essential Resource

Rose Dawson's Book Journals

My Time With The Fairies

Enchanted Escapades

Enchanted Escapades

Dewey Decimal Diaries

Siren's Songbook

Pride and Prejudice

Bibliophile's Bounty

Book of Books Journal

Pages & Passages Reading Journal

Bookworm's Companion Reading Journal & Tracker

ABOUT THE AUTHOR

Jax Wilder is a passionate romance author hailing from a charming small town nestled in the picturesque Pacific Northwest. With a heart full of love and an unyielding belief in the power of happily ever afters, Jax weaves enchanting tales of love and connection that leave readers captivated.

Jax's novels are a reflection of her commitment to celebrating the magic of love, and her characters' journeys mirror the warmth and happiness she has found in her own life. Join her on the enchanting journey of love, passion, and enduring connection through her heartfelt romance novels.

www.ingramcontent.com/pod-product-compliance
Lightning Source LLC
Chambersburg PA
CBHW030341120726
47901CB00007B/1868